Also by Ray Ordorica

The Alaskan Retreater's Notebook
Border Caper
Caracas Caper
Sixty Years of Testing Guns

CASABLANCA CAPER

by
Ray Ordorica

Cover photo "Charles Daly HP"
and cover design by Ray Ordorica

ISBN: 978-1-7331352-2-1

SHEEP CREEK PUBLISHING
NORTH FORK, IDAHO

This book is dedicated to the memory of Homer, my best friend and beloved companion over the past decade.

Requiescat In Pace, amigo.

This is a work of fiction. Other than a few real persons mentioned, all the characters in this book are fictitious. Except for some real names used in a fictitious manner, any similarity to persons living or dead is purely coincidental and unintentional. As always, if your name closely resembles any of the characters in this book you have our deepest sympathy.

ACKNOWLEDGEMENTS

My sincere thanks go out to my old friend Bruce Nourse for his guidance and advice given generously to the author on the subject of robotics machinery and particularly about the computers that drive them. Everything about computers that I got right in this book is thanks to Bruce. The blunders are mine.

Thanks to my buddy Danny Daniels for his wonderful words of encouragement during tough times along the path, and for his suggestion to 'drive' the California Route One.

Another shout-out goes to my Australian friend Tony Hadjion for his insight into the ongoing intrigues the Australian people have with the Chinese, who have serious footholds in Oz. Tony also educated me about the hierarchy of government secret services there, such as the ASIO.

TABLE OF CONTENTS

CHAPTER 1
Glitches

It was spring and Rico Morgan sat with his cat Homer under the apple tree as the bold breeze stirred the lilacs and gently wafted their heavenly, heady scent to him, overpowering the smoke of his stogie. A Harley farted up the road heading north. It bore its rider past Rico's small east-Idaho ranch toward colder weather up and over the border with Montana, and its noise roused Rico from his lethargy enough to peer once again at Ruxton's *Life in the Far West,* which he'd been reading on the warm and windy day until he nearly fell asleep. Homer lay drowsing, all fat and happy on a low little table in front of Rico's Adirondack chair.

The spring rain grew the grass fast and the wildflowers and dandelions came up just as fast. Bees busy in the apple blossoms overhead – those flowers remaining which the wind had not yet stripped of their petals, making a white and gentle snowfall – sounded a soft and persistent background buzz, somehow comforting to the lonely private eye.

Sally, his girlfriend, was gone. She left him after a nasty fight, and Rico thought she was probably gone for good. His other close friends were out of the country, so no one and yet everyone was on his mind that day, and he felt largely out of sorts with the world.

It'd been a horrid winter with more snow than usual. The cold lingered and sank into the bones of man and beast, sank deep into the earth until finally the sun came and scared away the frigid days and colder nights. Long after the last snowfall a few touches of it lay here and there where the sun was reluctant, until the warm air turned it into manna for the awakening grass.

The smoke from Rico's cigar, a fine H. Upmann Polo, swirled unpredictably in the sporadic breeze. A few early bugs clung to every advantage they could find, new wings not yet dry enough to give trustworthy flight, and that included clinging to Rico's sleeve. He let them cling. After all, it was close to Easter.

"If Christ could rise from the dead," thought Rico, "I can surely let a few desperate bugs hang onto my sleeve."

It would soon be summer, nearly a year after the events of Caracas, and Rico just wanted to be left alone. There was enough Presidente brandy and some decent Scotch still in his larder. There were plenty of good cigars in his humidor. His cats were fat and happy...maybe too fat. It was nice to just sit and smoke and relax.

He had enough money, so he didn't really want to go back to his special kind of work. Rico and Modesto, aka Mole, had been paid in gold bars at the outcome of a job they did for a top politician in Caracas the previous summer. A third gold bar went to Rico's friend Roxy Roades, the three of them having done the job together for the Venezuelan politician. In light of the lousy currency in Venezuela at the time, the politician offered the gold and it was gladly accepted. Each of the three got a one-kilo gold bar.

Rico's gold bar went into his vault. At the moment he had no need to turn it to cash, "Especially as the price of gold keeps threatening to go up," he explained to Sally when she wondered why he planned to just sit on the gold bar. "Eileen thinks it'll get to over $1,500 an ounce in a year." Eileen Tudarite was the financial expert at Boise Control, Rico's group of advisers and researchers that helped him get jobs.

Rico Morgan was an exclusive private eye in his late thirties. He looked like a thin version of Chuck Norris with some James Coburn thrown in. His long hair was sandy with touches of gray, and his blue eyes had crinkles at the corners when he smiled, which was not often. His clients were governments and others with relatively high financial capabilities. Rico had a consulting group consisting of five part-time people. The group was called Boise Control, and it kept an eye on the Internet and other news sources for potential jobs, problems of a sort that Rico and his assistants could solve. The jobs needed to involve sufficient money to pay everybody. Otherwise Rico stayed home and smoked cigars outdoors with his cats, sampled the brandy, and occasionally howled at the moon.

Boise Control's unofficial leader was I. Yeats Prunzalot, a man with vast computer skills and an equal amount of hacking genius. The oldest member of Boise Control was George William (G. Willie) Kers, a retired Chrysler executive with important connections worldwide. Willie liked cigars and older, hotter Chrysler products, one of which he found for Rico in the form of an immaculate dark-green V-6 twin turbo six-speed Dodge Stealth R/T.

Boise Control included Myrtle Stockwood, an ex-hooker who knew people and could psychoanalyze them faster and better than most high-dollar shrinks. Eileen Tudarite, whom we've already met, was the financial wizard of the group. She made a fortune on Wall Street and brought her skills to the Control group.

The gal with the unlikely but genuine name of Kikkan DaKrotch was in her mid-twenties and came to the U.S. from Holland to attend college. She had great intuitive insight into world politics and the people who controlled most of it.

The five people of Boise Control went looking for jobs for Rico, but sometimes a potential client would contact the group and ask Rico to get involved. That is what happened in the last two jobs taken on by Rico Morgan and company. The first of those was from U.S. Immigration and Customs Enforcement, ICE, which asked Rico to look into a series of murders at the New Mexican border, that story detailed in *Border Caper*. One of the top politicians in Caracas asked Rico and his Boise group to find a murderer and thief who disrupted the best-laid plans of the politician. That tale was told in *Caracas Caper*.

Rico lived in east Idaho some distance north of Salmon. His girlfriend Sally Foarth, an internationally known concert violinist, lived near him. Rico's friend Modesto Pincata Buena, whom everyone knew as Mole, was Mexican born and a U.S. citizen. He lived in New Mexico not far from Las Cruces. When duty called in the form of a job Rico agreed to take on, Mole often came along to help solve the problems and keep an eye on Rico's back. Mole was currently dating a woman he met on the last job, a musician named Cassie Saint John, also ex-patriate Mexican, who lived in Colorado near Denver.

"Homer, why doesn't something good fall from the sky and relieve us of our boredom."

Homer opened an eye, squeaked something in cat-ese, turned over and went back to sleep.

"That's not helping, *amigo*. Where's your fat cousin Louie? Is he after the Scotch again?" Rico stood up, stretched, put his book down, and thought about taking a walk, but then he heard a truck engine slowing down as the vehicle approached his driveway. The brown UPS truck pulled in, Homer disappeared at high speed around the corner of the house, and the driver delivered a large package into Rico's hands. As the truck pulled out of the drive Rico took the box to a table next to his outdoors 'throne' under the apple tree.

He didn't recognize the return address, which was Luftin-Borlew Industries out of Atlanta, so he opened the package with caution. Nothing exploded. No gases came out. Carefully packed inside the box was what appeared to be an intricate child's toy in the form of a small humanoid robot, somewhat less than two feet tall. A folder or booklet was also inside the box, with a note on its cover: "READ THIS FIRST!" Rico opened the booklet, leaving the robot inside the box.

The booklet was addressed to him.

It read, "Mr. Morgan, I was referred to you by the people at something called Boise Control, which entity realized I was having a problem, contacted me, and indicated maybe they, and you, could help. Please take careful note of the enclosed robotic humanoid. Do not switch it on before reading all of the notes here or the item might be damaged. It also might do some damage to you if you fail to observe necessary precautions."

Rico took a careful look at the thing in the box before he continued reading the booklet. "Well, kids," he addressed the birds and the bees, "I don't see no guns, no knives, nor any bags of poison, but I ain't gonna turn that thing on, or even touch it before I find out what the dickens this is."

The note continued. "You have perhaps not heard of my company. I am Herbert Harumfer, CEO of Luftin-Borlew. We provide robotics to many industries including Amazon, Ford Motor Company, Tesla, Inc., and a few others. Our equipment is considered to be some of the best in the industry. Recently we began to have problems with some of our robots, some of them being those nearest, or closely adjacent to, the human personnel in the various areas and industries where our equipment is deployed. The problems have been entirely random, and seem to be caused by outside interference of the sort that could be traced to unauthorized signals delivered to the computers that control our robotics. This caused their normal programming to be overridden. In each case serious damage was done to the material on which the robot in question was working. In two cases a human worker near the machine was injured, one severely.

"The enclosed humanoid robot will give you a demonstration of this programming failure. The robot is programmed to do certain things. When activated, it is supposed to stand up, walk ten paces, jump in the air, return five paces, stop and spin. I've sent it to you so you can personally see the 'glitches' in its performance. It doesn't do quite what we programmed it to do, and we cannot figure out why. It seems to do different things every time it's used."

Rico looked again at the figure in the box, but was still reluctant to touch it.

The note continued, "You might think it would be simple to block an incoming signal from, say, an overhead satellite. However, in all cases the affected robotics machinery is not connected to any online source, just like this humanoid example in the box. That would seem to preclude any sort of hacking via satellite, Internet, or other connectivity source. Wi-Fi and Bluetooth, etc., also do not seem to play a part here.

"We have tried to isolate the machinery, but it seems like our internal programming is becoming infected by some sort of discrete virus of unknown origin. It occurred to us the spurious signals might be instantly downloaded from a burst of energy from some outside source which somehow addresses our software and is then shut off. That is, once the damage is done and the spurious signal received, there is no need to continue any connection between our robots and the damaging source, whatever the latter may be. Yet so far as we can determine there are no outside connections to any of the robotics in question.

"We can occasionally discover and temporarily correct, but never entirely eliminate what I'm calling the *virus*, once it's infected the programming of our robot. Only by a complete reboot of the program is this possible, but in all instances the reboot did not completely free the virus from our programming. The robot would work properly for a short time, but the virus always comes back.

"As may be expected, the ongoing problems with our robotics are beginning to hurt our retail business. At this time our revenues are down twenty percent from last year's. Our prime competitor is Fortune Technologies, and even though it is a much smaller company and is located outside the United States, it is already reaping significant benefits from our ongoing problems. Other companies are also making headway against our formerly steadfast customers.

"It is my hope that you and your team can look into this and find a) the source of the trouble and b) a way to entirely eliminate future occurrences of this problem. May I please hear from you? Thank you for your time."

The rest of the notes indicated how to turn on the robotic figure, diagrams of what it was supposed to do, photographic images of the figure in action, and various contact sources so Rico could give the CEO his thoughts on the problem. There was even a return label so Rico could return the robot to the company.

With some trepidation Rico pulled the figure out of the box. It was limp, like a doll. He gave it a close inspection to see if it contained hidden knives, potential gun ports and the like. Following the instructions he turned the figure onto its face on the ground and opened a small door in its back. Inside were two switches labeled '1' and '2.' He flipped the switches in the proper order and stepped back from the robotic doll. A whir of machinery came from the device. It became 'alive' and stood up. It was about eighteen inches tall.

"Looks like Howdy Doody," thought Rico. "Wrong clothes, tho."

The head swiveled, the eye-like cameras on its face picked out a clear path and the robot began to move. It took ten paces, stopped, jumped into the air about six inches, turned around and headed back. It was supposed to stop after five paces and, according to the information given, spin, presumably like a dancer. Instead, when it got to the five-pace position it leaped into the air at least a foot off the ground, made a half a turn and began running across Rico's yard until it crashed into the side of his house, fell to the ground, and emitted a grinding sound as its legs continued to thrash. Rico turned it off.

"Well, that was fun," Rico said to no one. "So now what do I do?" Rico thought about it, and remembered the note said different things sometimes happened to the robot. He decided to run it again. He again put it face down on the ground, flipped the switches and stood back. This time the small humanoid robot stood up, looked around, found a clear path and took the ten paces. Then it stopped, attempted to walk backwards, fell over, righted itself and stood up again, took ten paces, spun around, and stood still. Rico was about to turn it off when the thing leaped into the air, spun again, and dashed off into the side of the house again.

Rico turned it off, put the thing back into the box and returned to his chair. He fired up his neglected cigar and stared at nothing for a long time.

Eventually Homer the cat returned cautiously from hiding to keep Rico company in his brown study.

"Homer, my boy, I don't know anything at all about robotics and the software that drives it. I know a little about free-style robotics dance, thanks to that incredibly talented and extremely lovely Sarah 'Lil' Mini' Phoenix girl on Instagram, but I don't think she'll help me with this problem. But I *do* know someone who knows all about robotics, and that's my old friend Bruce Nourse in Ann Arbor. I think a phone call to him might help. Whatta ya think, son?"

Homer said nothing.

"Okay, I'll do it. Thanks, buddy."

CHAPTER 2
Mysteries

Rico had attended college at the University of Michigan in Ann Arbor. He made lots of friends in that town and many of them were still in touch with him. One of these was Bruce Nourse, with whom Rico made a lot of guitar and singing music in their time together at the U. of M. After college Bruce made his living writing software for robotics in many fields. If anyone could help Rico with this problem it was Bruce. Rico dialed his number.

"Hi, this is Rico Morgan. Long time no talk. How's your airplane going?" Rico knew Bruce owned a Cessna 172 but didn't know he'd just sold it.

"Sold! I got tired of paying hangar fees, and there were a few other little problems with it, so it's out the door. The good news is I can rent it any time I want to. It sold locally."

"That's great! I sold my Citabria too a while back, and it went off to California. Sold it for the same reasons, in fact. Hangar fees are indeed nasty. I got tired of flying around the local valley just to exercise the airplane and maybe do a few simple stunts with it. You know, it's the old story about an airplane being a hole in the air into which you throw money."

"You mean a hole in the hangar into which you throw money. So why the call? Are you in the process of solving a mystery you can't handle, and need my considerable help?"

"Actually, yes. I'm considering getting involved with a mystery concerning software within a robotics company that seems to be giving them fits. The company is Luftin-Borlew Industries, which makes robotics for Elon Musk, Bezos's company Amazon, and a few others. The software seems to be getting buggered to the point where it's unreliable for the tasks at hand and dangerous to the operator or inspector standing near it. What I need to know is how these computers are getting hacked when they're not connected to the Internet. Can you shed any light?"

"Rico, there's no way anything can get into the software unless it's hooked to the Internet somehow. The only other way for the software to get damaged would be for someone local to stick a thumb drive or CD into the computer that connects with the machinery."

"How about a strong signal from a satellite that might get into it?"

"No. It's impossible for a satellite to send a signal that can disrupt the machinery without some physical connection. Now, that physical connection might be from something like Wi-Fi or a few other local-area connectibles, and there's half a dozen. But the computer has to be set to receive those signals. The robotics computer is generally isolated from such signals to avoid the problems you've described."

"So," replied Rico, "it's gotta be either a local bit of malware stuck into it by somebody near the machinery, or there's a surreptitious Internet connection?"

"That's it. You might have a bad guy on the scene, but that seems unlikely from what you said about three or four companies and several machines at each company being affected."

"I agree. The likelihood of all those people wanting to jeopardize their jobs and who also would have a grudge against the company is not very big."

"Well, Rico," said Bruce, "you might've hit on a clue there. Look for someone with a grudge against the company, or against its owners. That might be a starting place."

"Excellent idea. Thanks. Also, if you come up with any way the computers can be externally buggered without a physical contact, please let me know."

"Roger that. Bye!"

Rico next phoned I. Yeats Prunzalot in Boise, acting and unofficial head of Rico's Boise Control operation. "Yeats, thanks for ferreting out a job for me. I just had contact from the gentleman CEO of Luftin-Borlew, the troubled company. I hope we can do something with this."

"Oh dearie me!" Yeats spoke with a heavy Indian accent. His 'dearie' sounded like 'ditty.' "I was going to tell you about this potential new job, kind sir, but I forgot. My sincere apologies!"

"No problem, Yeats. I was bored here, so this is good." Rico then posed the question to him. "Yeats, is there any way a computer can be hacked by an outside source without any physical contact?"

"Indeedy that is so, Mr. Morgan. Signals can be installed into a computer via Wi-Fi and similar signal senders. Of course the computer has to have its core set to receive these signals."

"Okay, I knew that. What else?"

"There are other methods such as interwire connectivity, which uses the existing power lines in a house or office, but this again requires special equipment to be installed, so the knowledge of its existence, the presence of this network that runs using existing wiring, would be known by the owners. Then of course there is the data that can be obtained through side-channel analysis, which usually requires close-proximity access to the hardware of the computer, but this generally is used to take data or information off the computer, not put anything onto it. A typical nasty use would be to get a password off a smart card to permit the card's use by someone besides its owner, as in stealing money from someone's bank account, and the like."

"Can you explain that a bit?" Rico was in the dark.

"Every electronic device gives off a sort of impulse or signature of its operation, no matter what is it. For example, if you turn on a radio or television set near your computer you may get interference in the radio or TV signal from the electronics doing their work inside your computer. Those interference transmissions, which go through the air, not through the wires, are complex, especially from the components, chips and things, that make up the computer, but it is possible for equally complex devices to read those signals. In a recent test a password was typed on a computer in one room and a reception device in the next room was able to read the password from the emissions given off by the first keyboard. There may have been some slight alterations to the 'sending' keyboard, but you get the idea. Given sufficient time, proper technology, and desire, a lot of information can be obtained through the air waves with no connection. In fact some of today's 'smart cards' have no electronic connection at all."

"Yeats," replied Rico, "my credit card was hacked some years ago, apparently while I was standing in line at a grocery store. Is that the sort of thing you're describing?"

"Yes indeedy. The advances in remote-scanning ability made over the years since your card was hacked has led to the introduction of so-called 'chips' in the credit cards, which make that sort of thing harder to accomplish. But it's still easy for someone with the right knowledge and equipment to get the data off your card at almost a glance, so the so-called added security of the chip is largely bogus."

"Hmm," replied Rico. "That's scary, but that concept doesn't seem to be able to get a malicious signal back onto the computers in question, does it? Let me explain in detail the problem as it was presented to me, and perhaps you can look into it and see if we can do anything about this. Looks to be lucrative, so I hope so, but not if we remain in the dark."

Rico told Yeats about the small humanoid robot sent to him, and read the note from the CEO of the troubled company.

"So that's all I know at this time, my friend. Could you please dig into this and see if we can tackle it?"

"Yes indeedy," replied Yeats. "I will check my sources today and I will let you know what I can find."

"Thanks, Yeats. Give my regards to your dad."

Later that day Yeats called Rico and gave him new information. "Mr. Morgan, another thing occurred to me in this computer problem. It is possible that a component, such as the main computer chip that makes up the basic control interface of the computer, on the so-called motherboard, has been programmed with malicious information with a time-set signal, which means after a certain amount of time or perhaps after a certain number of particular oscillations, or cycles, or signals occur, the malware takes over and changes the programmed operation. That might explain what is happening here."

"I think I understand," replied Rico. "If, say, a logic chip is preset to do one thing for say a few thousand cycles and then switches modes and does something different, there would be no way of knowing about it beforehand."

"That is correct.," replied Yeats. "So if the Luftin-Borlew company is purchasing its computer components from someone or some company that is capable of installing this time-delayed corruption, that might answer your problem. It seems to me you might begin to look into who would want to do that to this company."

"Thanks, Yeats. I'm already thinking about that. Do you have any information on the owners or other headmen of the company?"

"Mr. Boris Luftin and Charles P. Borlew were the founders. Both went to MIT at about the same time, and began the company a decade ago. It was successful from the start. Mr. Borlew passed away prematurely three years ago and the sole owner of the company today is Mr. Luftin, and of course the stockholders. Luftin holds a majority of the stock, so he's 'the man.' He has little to do with the running of the company and largely acts as its spokesman. The gentleman who contacted you, Herbert Harumfer, attended college at Northwestern, and is essentially in charge of the daily operations as CEO. He has been with the company since its beginning."

"So I'm looking for anyone or any company that might today have a grudge against Boris Luftin or maybe Hoibie Harumfer, the CEO. Thanks Yeats. Please see if you can find anything on them."

"I am already doing that, kind sir, and might have some information in a day or two."

CHAPTER 3
Murder

"Dead. Dead as a doornail. Been dead a while from the rigor and the smell." Inspector Ralf Raktum of the Atlanta Police Department spoke to Mitzi Grazer, the head of forensics as she came into the room. The room was a huge, dark and comfortable library with oak paneling, thick carpets, three of the walls lined with books, a fancy walnut desk, a couple of chairs, TV screen, a few wall hangings between bookshelves and other typical amenities of the library of a wealthy man. "Bleedin' locked room. No one in it but our victim, no way to get in except through the door or the windows which are all closed and locked; yet he's dead. There's no obvious sign of violence. Take a look."

"That's what I'm here for, Ralf." Mitzi Grazer glared at the Inspector with a jaded eye. She knew Ralf Raktum's friend Billy Barkter wanted to be top dog in forensics but didn't quite cut it with the local politicos who placed the top people in that job. They put Mitzi in charge, Inspector Raktum didn't like it, and he held a grudge against Mitzi ever since. And she knew it. It was over two years now since she was appointed, and in all that time the Inspector never said one kind word to Mitzi. He tried always to point out her shortcomings, or so it seemed to her.

She took a look at the victim. "What's this guy's name?" she asked of the room full of police.

"He's Herbert Harumfer, CEO of Luftin-Borlew Industries in nearby Atlanta." A cop on the scene responded to Mitzi's question. "One of his people from the company came looking when Herbie didn't show up at the office for three days and wouldn't respond to his phone. He lives alone, no servants. The company man knocked, got no response, and because he saw Herbie's car in the garage he circled the house. When he got to that window there, looking in here on the library, he saw Herbie slumped over his desk, face down on his laptop. Called 911 and here we are."

"Thanks, Dale," said Mitzi. "We've got all our photos, then? Okay, I'm gonna look closer at this guy." She pried his head up off the laptop and peered at his face and his eyes. "Blue skin...suffocation apparent," she said into her pocket recorder. "Rictus indicates pain. Clutching fingers ditto. Vomiting apparent. Could be poison gas. No almond smell detected. I suspect Sarin. Laptop computer still running. Victim's face was lying on it when found. Okay, you guys can get this body out of here now." A crew came and removed the quite stiff stiff from the library, leaving the desk with its laptop essentially clear.

"What's the computer doing? Anything obvious?" Dale the cop asked as he approached the desk.

Mitzi responded, "It's set to his email account, apparently. Unless his head changed it when he took a dive."

"What the hell?" Dale looked over Mitzi's shoulder and stared at the computer screen. "Is that for real?" Behind the initial window for the email-message page the little bit of background screen behind it seemed to be fluttering.

"What the hell?" repeated Mitzi.

"We may not want to turn that thing off," said Dale. "Might be a clue hidden in the background blinking. I've got some computer experience with viruses and that looks like one I saw a few months ago. You might want to document all that, maybe with a video recording, before you shut it down."

"Good idea, Dale. Curt!" She hollered at one of her crew across the room. "Bring a video camera over here, if you please."

Curt brought the camera and a small tripod. Mitzi set up the camera and made a recording of the computer screen bouncing in the background.

Inspector Raktum returned to the library from a brief tour of the house. "Not a soul around," he said to the room, "and no indication of any servants or even visitors here. He must've lived completely alone."

Mitzi said, "Inspector, you might want to see this."

He walked over to the desk and asked, "What gives? Er...what the hell?" He saw the blinking images behind the email window.

"That seems to be the question of the hour," said Mitzi. "I think an email message triggered something here and caused the image flow you see back there behind this window." She made the email window smaller so more of the background was visible. "That action makes the laptop get hot. Hear the fans blowing?"

"Yeh. So did this guy die from a hot laptop? Maybe got hypnotized from the images? What do you think?" Ralf asked her.

"Inspector, I think it's suspicious, but right now it's kind of a hazy deal. Might be a clue here somewhere, though. I've got it recorded on video so we can look at it later if need be."

"Good work, Miss Grazer."

"Please call me Mitzi," she said as a way of acknowledging the first kind thing Ralf Raktum ever said to her.

"They're repeating." This from Ralf after he watched for half a minute.

After a short while it became obvious that the images there were indeed repeating, showing the same ones over and over, continually keeping the processor chip of the laptop working hard. The fans made a low-grade howling from air movement and spinning motors. Mitzi felt the air escaping from the unit making a gentle breeze into the face of whoever was using the machine.

"You guys notice the wind in the face?" Mitzi asked her fellow workers. "Why is that? Isn't it supposed to be directed towards the back, away from whoever's using it?"

Dale the cop said, "That's not normal. Air usually goes out the back and sides. That avoids blowing hot air into the face of the operator. This ain't right."

"The laptop's plugged into the wall," said Mitzi, "so the thing's still running. If it was on battery power the whole thing would be as dead as Herbie by now," she said. "Once we get it to the lab we can see if there's anything odd about it. I see three days ago it downloaded a message from...Billie Blogger. Sounds phony. Before that someone named Rico Morgan sent a message to this computer. Lengthy." She scanned Rico's note. "It seems to be about computer hacking, apparently. Inspector, you might want to check out this email." She pointed to the note from Rico Morgan, second-to-last message on the machine.

Inspector Ralf Raktum read the message, made a few notes, and copied the contact information Rico sent to the dead CEO.

"By the way, what's this thing?" Ralf pointed to the Wi-Fi router next to the desk.

"That's a router," said Mitzi. "Lets him connect to the Internet anywhere he wants to carry that laptop. It also means anyone in range can hack into his emails and find out what he's doing."

"How's that?" asked Ralf.

"Well, f'r instance someone could have read that note from Rico Morgan as they sat in a car outside the grounds of this place."

"Ah. Indirect hacking, I guess," said Ralf.

"That's it. Wi-Fi leaves you open to that."

Mitzi kept her video camera running as she closed the email program's window and watched the blinking window behind it. The repeating images slowed and finally stopped, and after a minute the fans slowed also. She pulled the plug on the laptop and put the video camera away.

"Okay," she said. "It begins to look like this laptop might be the killer of our Herbie. Bag it up, guys, and do it carefully. Whatever killed him might have left some deadly traces in the laptop."

Rico Morgan's phone rang. "Mr. Morgan, this is Chief Inspector Ralf Raktum with the Atlanta Police Department. Might I have a word with you?"

"Yes, of course," replied Rico. "What's up?"

"We're investigating the murder of Herbert Harumfer in Atlanta and would like to ask you a few questions."

"Ah. So that's why I haven't heard back from him. Sure, go ahead."

"We inspected his laptop and found an email from you to him that was somewhat unusual. It indicates you got a package from him and that you were temporarily stumped about the presumed hacking of his computers, but would pursue it and get back to him in the next week or so. Your email included your contact information, hence my phone call."

"Yes, that's pretty much what I said. He sent me a package containing a small robot which demonstrated the problems his company's been having with their industrial robotics, which I believe are sold to Tesla, Amazon, Ford, and a few other high-dollar companies. He wanted me and my people to look into what might be causing the trouble with the computers that drive the robotics. That's somewhat out of my sphere of knowledge, but I have a team here that can examine the problem quite completely, we're sure, given time and sufficient information. I tried to convey that idea to Mr. Harumfer."

"I see," replied Ralf. "You were talking about industrial computers, not personal laptops."

"That's correct. May I ask why you thought a personal laptop was involved?"

"Mr. Morgan, it looks like Herbert Harumfer was hacked to death by his own laptop."

Boris Luftin, the remaining founder of Luftin-Borlew Industries, had just received the information his CEO was dead. He sat in his study absently scanning the Internet and pondering who might be able to replace Herbert Harumfer, the recently deceased CEO. He barely heard the distant buzz of his front door's bell.

Boris Luftin's maid answered the doorbell and admitted two uniformed police officers. They asked to see Mr. Luftin and the maid showed them to his study, where he was squinting at his laptop computer. Dale Coburn, the same cop who was with Mitzi Grazer in the study of the late Herbert Harumfer, saw Luftin busy on his laptop and immediately said, "Mr. Luftin, stop what you're doing right now and step away from your computer."

Boris, who had lifted his head when the officers stepped into his study, said "What? What's the meaning of this? This is an outrage! You can't just barge into my house and order me around. Who are you? Why are you here?"

"We're the cops and we're ordering you to stand up right now, put your hands in the air, and step away from the desk and away from that computer. Do it now!" Dale barked out the last command, which got Boris' attention. He rose in his chair to comply.

One of the cops took him by the arm and pulled him firmly away from the desk before Boris could once again touch the laptop. Dale, the cop in charge, went to the desk and, with blue rubber gloves on, carefully closed the laptop, unplugged the power cable, inserted it into a heavy polyester bag, sealed the bag, and put that bag inside a second airtight bag which he also sealed.

With the computer in the bags he made to leave the room with the other cop, who released Luftin once the laptop was captured inside the bags.

"You bastards! I've got important stuff on that computer. Give it back!"

Dale glared at the man and asked him, "Is it more important than your life?"

"What the hell?" was all Luftin could say.

"Mr. Luftin, we're sorry to have to do this, but we found out the nearly identical computer that was being used by Mr.

Harumfer is what killed him. Where did you get this computer?" Dale waited for the answer.

"Ah, ah, ah," stammered Luftin, "it was a gift from...I forgot who now, some charity to whom we donated a bunch of dollars a few years ago. I got one, and so did Harumfer. Might have been one or two more gifted out, I forget now. Killed how?"

"Harumfer's laptop held a poison capsule that was triggered by an email sent to him. Before you ask, we don't have a source for the email." Dale looked out the window. "Don't know who sent it, but the message triggered something in the laptop that resulted in Harumfer's death. We suspect your laptop, which looks like the same custom type that he had, might also contain that lethal setup."

"Can you preserve the information on the computer? I have some deals going that have their details on that laptop, matters of millions of dollars." Boris Luftin looked extremely worried.

"Yes, sir, we can preserve everything on it, all the data, but we have to be sure there's no deadly device stuck into it first."

"Well, then, I guess I owe you guys thanks, not curses. Who would do such a thing?"

"That, sir, is what we'd like to know too."

Luftin ran a hand through his thinning hair. "You say a virus sent to Herbie killed him? How did it work?"

Dale paused, considered, and responded. "It tripped something on the laptop. It caused the laptop to cycle on some endless task as the first step. That got the computer's main chip hot. Then the poison was released, which the fans blew into his face."

"Damn! And that's on my laptop too, you think?"

"It may be. Can you find out who else might've got these laptops as a gift?"

"Maybe. I can ask my secretary. She keeps notes on that sort of thing and might have some info. I'll let you know."

"The sooner the better, sir, and thank you for understanding."

Dale and the other cop took their leave.

Boris Luftin stared out his library window.

Rico was on the phone again to Yeats. "Apparently the laptop was fitted with a small capsule of Sarin gas," said Rico, "placed near or on top of the main chip, according to the police analysis in Atlanta. It was so well done, they told me, it could have been done by the manufacturer, but that seems highly unlikely. The dead man received an email that, first of all, forced the computer into a mode where it had to work on an endless task. It cycled all the photographic images in his 'My Pictures' file, and that caused the main chip in the laptop to heat up significantly. The heat caused the computer's cooling fans to run, but they had been redirected to blow the hot air into the face of the operator."

"That is not good," said Yeats.

Rico continued. "Then the email triggered the generation of a multi-tone sound, some five or six notes including two discords, the sort of stuff that normal music would never make. The notes were put through the speakers. Those discordant tones, acting through the normal speaker connection in the laptop, caused a small but potent battery to send a strong current through a nichrome wire. The battery was not part of the original laptop, but had been built into it along with the rest of the poisonous setup. This nichrome wire was wrapped around the plastic capsule of Sarin. The battery current made the nichrome wire glow red hot, and the hot wire caused the capsule to burst, which let the liquid Sarin drip directly down onto the hot processor chip. This, along with the heat from the hot wire, turned the liquid to gas and the computer's fans blew the gas into the man's face, thereby killing him.

Yeats said, "Of course the poison was not built into the laptop nor the chip by the manufacturer. That processor chip would have been used in tens of thousands of laptops. A computer-chip factory would have no reason to target tens of thousands of innocent buyers, each and all of them just waiting for a signal that would kill them. The only reasonable alternate is that somehow this deadly setup found its way into this specific man's laptop and was done by someone thoroughly familiar with computers. That means of course it was planted, perhaps by a repairman or by anyone else who had access to this laptop and wanted to be able to kill the user of the laptop at a moment's notice. Another possibility, Mr. Morgan, is that the laptop was presented to the dead man by someone who one day might want to kill him."

"Yeats, that might be the answer. A presentation gift, or the like. The cop in Atlanta said the computer looked extra fancy. Leather cover, stuff like that. It could've been a gift, and I'll have to look into that. Or the Atlanta police will, since we haven't been hired."

"I agree. Please keep me informed. I am, by the way, still looking into ways the industrial computers might have been attacked, in case we do get hired."

"Good idea, Yeats. I'll call you in a few days whether or not anyone calls."

Two days later Rico again phoned I. Yeats Prunzalot at Boise Control's main office in Boise, which was actually Yeats' home. "Yeats, we got the job. The factory owner Boris Luftin contacted me personally after he got briefed by the Atlanta cops about this deal. In addition to solving the computer glitch problems we've been hired to look into Herbie's death. I'm going to Atlanta tomorrow to talk with this Luftin fellow. Any suggestions about the hacking I might be able to tell him?"

"Not yet, Mr. Morgan. I have some ideas but have not yet finished testing them. I believe the clue is the side-channel technology, which may not be just unidirectional. That is what I am testing, but I need some more time."

"Okay, Yeats. I won't ask you to explain. Right now that's way over my head, so I won't mention it to Mr. Luftin. Did you happen to find out who might want to damage the company?"

"No, kind sir. With all my odd research and experimentation into the side-channel technology I have not had time to look into the personnel behind this company. However, I did ask my associates to see what they could find, but so far we have nothing. You might want to talk with Mr. Luftin about that. It could be that some person from his college days might be involved, even these many years after his time at university. Some grudges last a lifetime. Also, kind sir, please to ask him for the source of his main computer-controlling chips. That might be helpful to our inquiry."

"Okay, I'll be sure ask him where he buys the chips for his robotic stuff. That's an excellent idea." Rico thanked him, broke the connection, and continued packing for Atlanta.

CHAPTER 4
Confusion

"Who might have had a grudge against you, Mr. Luftin?" Rico Morgan, wearing his usual travel clothes consisting in a dark brown tweed sports jacket, dress shirt open at the collar with no tie but showing a black tee shirt underneath, black jeans and black shoes, sat in Boris Luftin's office at the headquarters of Luftin-Borlew Industries in Atlanta, Georgia.

Luftin sat behind a huge fancy-wood desk with a large window behind him. He was on the heavy side of fit, with a quizzical expression on his face and piercing black eyes. He wore a gray suit, red tie loose at the neck, and was clearly going bald. There was a fringe of graying hair just above his ears and a thin bit combed over the top. He spoke with a commanding voice. "Beats me! No one recently did anything to me or against me, so far as I know. Looking back a few years, the same thing applies. There's no one I can think of who might hold a grudge against me or against the company."

"How about back in college?"

"Oh, you're kidding! Who would hold a grudge that long? That's close to twenty years ago!"

"But there was someone, wasn't there?"

"Well...there might have been. An incident, long ago, at a campus bar...." Luftin's voice trailed off as he recalled the distant past.

"Can you tell me about it? What do you recall?" Rico encouraged the man.

"Heck, it can't be that! So stupid!"

"Let me have it."

"Okay." He sighed, sat back in his chair and stared out the window. "It happened back in college. I was a senior at MIT and doing well enough in my classes...Mechanical Engineering with a major, such as it was, in Manufacturing Processes. My soon-to-be business partner Chuck Borlew was in advanced computer programming. We didn't socialize together back then. Didn't really know each other 'til after college. Anyway, I was out at a local tavern one weekend, Saturday night break from my studies, having a beer. A buddy said he'd meet me there but he never showed, so I was just sittin' there alone. There was a mediocre band playing some sort of country crap. Then she walked in.

"A fat guy came in with a slim brunette, really lovely girl. Becky was her name, and she was badly pissed off at the fat guy. She saw me sitting alone, so she shook off Mr. Fat and came and sat with me. We talked. Bought her a beer. We hit it off right away. We kept on talking. The fat guy sat across the room from us and kept his eye on me and Becky. I could see he was getting pretty well looped, tossing down shots and beer. Becky didn't once look at him. We had our beer and kept on talking.

"Pretty soon the fat guy's had enough to drink, so he ups and walks over to our table. He grabs Becky by the arm and tries to pull her up and away from the table. I might not look it now, but I was on the school rowing team back then, so I was tough and flexible. I actually looked kinda wimpy. He must've thought I wouldn't put up any resistance. I stand up and Fatso takes a swing at me. I expected it, ducked, and he missed. I poked him in the chops a good one, grabbed him by the shoulder and seat of pants, and walked him right out of the bar, just threw him out into the street. When I got back to my seat everyone in the bar cheered me, and Becky was smiling. Apparently that chunky guy was not well liked by the folks at that bar, and I was the first one to stand up to him. He was pretty big, but soft and all bluff.

"Becky and I ended up getting married, and we're still married. I never saw nor heard from that fat guy again. I heard he transferred to another school right after that incident, and years later I heard he became successful in some business venture"

"What was his name?" Rico asked.

"Farchex. Something Farchex. I remember him because he was known as fat-cheeks because of his fat ass. Don't remember his first name."

"Well," said Rico, that's something. Do you remember any other incidents like that along the way?"

"Nope. Nothing. I can't imagine that guy would hold a grudge after all these years."

"I'll take a look into it and see if I can find out anything. Meantime, are any of your locations near any of the proposed 5G towers?"

"I have no idea. I can find out for you, if you think it's necessary."

"Please do so. My computer man tells me there's some capabilities built into the 5G technology that can update some computer stuff without any connection, but we're not fully up to snuff on it. But do check, because you never know. One more thing. Do you know the source of your main computer-controlling chips?"

"Actually we buy them from a large electronics clearing-house. I'm not sure who makes them. We look for the best deal because of the large numbers involved."

"I see. So they could come from anyone. I'm guessing your total sales units are so high you can't just replace 'em all."

"Replace them all? Good heavens, no! Anything else?"

"That's all I've got at the moment."

"Thank you, Mr. Morgan. Do you know when I can get my laptop back?"

"No, that's up to Atlanta PD," said Rico. "I know they found the same setup inside your laptop as in the one that killed Harumfer. The cops told me they're looking into another two or three of them that were gifted to some of your board members. Did you find out where they came from?"

"They came from Looky Dooky Toys for Tots, a company to which we donated some money as a community donation, a good-will gesture. They said they bought them from some source for which they had no records. This was over two years ago...nearly three."

"Well, Mr. Luftin, thank your lucky stars you didn't go out the same way as your CEO. Someone doesn't like your company."

"Why was Harumfer killed? Any ideas?"

Rico Morgan paused, staring at the rug for half a minute. "I think it was because he asked me and my people to look into this. If that's the case, you can expect the bad guys will either take some further action against you and your company – or against me and mine."

"Mr. Morgan, kind sir, I have some new information for you."

It was morning. Rico was having breakfast in his hotel room in Atlanta when the phone rang. He stood up to answer the nearby landline wall phone and it was Yeats at Rico's Boise Control operation. "What might you have, Yeats, kind sir?"

"The name you gave me, Farchex, belongs to one August X. Farchex, former student at MIT, later transferred to Northwestern University in mid-junior year. He is the owner and CEO of a company called Fortune Technologies. He makes...."

"Robotics," cut in Rico. "He's the guy that Luftin threw out of a bar some twenty years ago, stole his girl, and married her."

"That would seem to be the case, kind sir. It is possible he is the, er, fly in the ointment."

"Does he have any connection to the murder weapon, which was the laptop of Mr. Harumfer?"

"Possibly. His company also makes and markets commercial computer chips including an odd one that is sold to many toy companies and to a few laptop makers."

"A chip for toys?"

"Yes."

"What kind of toys?"

"I was hoping you would ask that, kind sir," replied Yeats in his thick accent. "The toys in question, and also some computer games, have what are marketed as 'random activities.' The toys do different things each time they are picked up and turned on, and the computer games operate along a similar line of thinking. Just when you think you have won a particular computer game the game switches, and you are either out of the game, or have to start from another angle to try to win it before it switches again. It seems to be somewhat of a cursed thing."

"Yeats, I think you just solved this whole problem. If these chips, or something like them, are put into a robotics computer and if the computer runs properly for a while and then switches because of one of these random-action chips, that would explain the glitches the Luftin-Borlew company is experiencing."

"That, kind sir, is the same conclusion to which I have arrived."

"So Farchex at Fortune Technologies is apparently making these random-activity chips. Anyone else?"

"Yes indeedy. There is another company, in this country. It is a small and new concern, named Fission Chips. It is in Illinois."

"Where is Fortune Technologies based, Yeats?"

"Morocco."

"Morocco? North Africa?"

"Actually in Casablanca."

"Good grief!" Rico sat down. I suppose you want me to go over there to question him. Is there any way we can do that without sending me to Africa?"

"At this time, sir, we really don't have enough information for you to go there. My associates and I are looking into every aspect of the company. Our Mr. William Kers has some old friends in Portugal, a little over two hundred miles by air across the Mediterranean from Morocco, and he may be able to discover something about that company through his friends."

"Is there any love, or any good reason, to look into the other company, the, er...Fission Chips outfit?"

"I have Kikkan doing that now, kind sir. She is researching it on the Internet. So far all she has found is that the company is small and located in the Chicago area. They provided some of the random chips to a computer gaming company, but not to any toys. It is apparently easier to get a chip to modify a game than to move parts of a physical toy randomly. We suspect the real villain is the Morocco-based Fortune Technologies."

"Okay. Please keep me posted with anything you find out about these odd chips. Any word from the Atlanta PD about the killer laptops?"

"Not at this time. They are chasing down two more of them but one of the two owners gave the laptop away and the other moved to a different state."

Rico replied, "It's vital we find those laptops before someone else buys the farm through one of 'em. I'll try to get the locals onto that. Thanks, Yeats"

Rico cut the connection and walked to the hotel window. He looked out at the city of Atlanta, seeing all that was in front of him but registering not much of anything. The fact that, but for Yeats and the gang in Boise, he was pretty well alone in the world at that time struck him hard, but he could do nothing about it.

Rico left the hotel and took a long walk, eventually finding himself near a diner, and as it was early afternoon he went in and got himself some sausage and eggs, a cup of coffee, toast and marmalade with butter. And he still felt like crap. He didn't know what was going on with this murder and computer mess and, worse, had no one to talk with. He finished his lunch, paid the tab with a good tip to the waitress, and left into the hot sun of Atlanta.

Across from the diner Rico spotted a park and decided to continue his walking and thinking in there.

An hour later Rico still felt morose and found himself on a park bench alone. It being a weekday in a busy city not many people were parading around the park, which suited his mood.

Rico's thoughts turned back to early summer, to the fight he'd had with Sally. It all seemed so stupid, so unnecessary. If they'd both kept their mouths shut....

CHAPTER 5
The Fight

But maybe it had been necessary. It bothered him all the way home from Caracas on the 'highjacked' jetliner, and it bothered him later at his tiny ranch when the group gathered to discuss all that had happened in Venezuela. Rico, Mole, Roxy Roades the CIA agent, Rico's violinist girlfriend Sally Foarth and three other musicians all flew out of troubled Caracas on what one of the musicians described as a highjacked airliner. The airplane had Aeromexico markings on the fuselage, but flew them from Caracas directly to El Paso. When the group boarded in Caracas the airplane was filled with 'passengers' that looked to Rico like mercenaries. They were all tough, youngish men, ready for action. They never had to leave their seats, as it transpired, at the Caracas airport, and they stayed to themselves all the long flight from Caracas to El Paso. From El Paso Rico, Mole, Sally, Roxy, and one of the Mexican violinists named Cassie Saint John caught another oddly convenient flight from El Paso directly to Missoula, and were then taken in a private limo straight from Missoula to Rico's ranch in east Idaho. The group gathered there for several days to discuss everything, play some music, and share their thoughts and emotions about the massive troubles in Caracas.

Nothing was said about the bogus Aeromexico jetliner or the convenient flight to Missoula or the convenient limousine right to Rico's front door, but it nagged Rico all during the journey and all during the week-long visit of the friends to Rico's ranch and Sally's nearby house. Questions burned in Rico's mind.

"How in hell does my lady friend Sally, the fine fiddler, go about getting together with a clandestine group to fly in a private, falsely marked jet plane into the heart of Caracas, play fiddle with three other people for several days, and then fly home on the private jet with them, adding me, Mole, Roxy, and our three gold bricks, no questions asked? Nobody had tickets. It was a bogus airliner, but who owns it? Why was the airliner filled with fairly obvious mercenaries posing as passengers? The setup looks to me like big government had a massive hand in it. It makes sense only if Sally is a member of some big-government group. Hell, if they'd asked her to go play a wedding for some bozo's daughter in Caracas just because she's a good fiddler, she'd turn 'em down. Too dangerous! She'd reject the proposal – unless she was part of a team that normally did that sort of stuff.

"So, what team? CIA? Nah, Roxy would've said something. But Roxy did say she knew Sally in DC. I know Sally stops in DC before every tour she makes with her priceless fiddle. She says it's to get the paperwork all fixed so there'll be no problems getting the violin in and out of wherever she's going. She goes to some strange countries. Even went to Russia a few years ago. Could she be gathering info for the U.S. government on her visits? Sure, she could! Why not?! She hobnobs with the highest government officials who attend her concerts. Why not just ask a few discrete questions an innocent violinist might ask? Or a government spook? Who would suspect her of being some sort of agent? Besides me...."

Rico had to ask Sally.

He agonized over it for a long time, but couldn't come up with a better solution than to just spit it out and see what happened. He was sometimes dumb that way. Speak his mind and the devil take the consequences. "What harm can it do?" he thought. "We love each other. How can she have this big secret from me? I tell her everything – except about Roxy and me. I don't tell her that. I *can't* tell her that. Could she *know* already? I sure as hell hope not! But she can tell me everything, can't she? Let's find out."

After Roxy and Mole and Cassie left for their own homes, Rico decided to ask Sally. The first morning coffee they had together alone, at Sally's home, Rico dumped it out.

"Sally, I know you didn't just wing over to Caracas on a whim. I know you'd never go there with that group unless you had to. Can you please tell me what gives here? What government group are you part of?"

Sally hesitated a long time, and finally admitted, with a soft, unhappy voice, while looking at the floor, "I'm a part-time spy. I have been since well before we got together. I sometimes use my fiddling concerts to find out stuff if I can, about the countries I go to and the people I meet along the way. It's nothing big, just something I do to get extra cash and make life more interesting other than just traveling and playing."

"My girlfriend is a freakin' spy and I never knew it. So you're a spook...and you never told me?! Why did you keep this secret from me? I don't have any secrets from you. Why do you...."

"No secrets? Bullshit," Sally replied, cutting Rico off with a dramatically rising voice. "I know damned well you and Roxy are fucking. It was written all over your faces when she showed up at your place after you came to rescue me in England. I made a joke about it and you and she nearly glowed in the dark, you both got so red. You both could hardly walk with your sore crotches. So what other secrets are *you* keeping from *me*? Asshole!"

"Goddammit, we're not married!" Rico nearly shouted this. "And who the hell do you work for in the government? CIA? NSA? That's a serious load of crap to keep that from me. A heluva lot more serious than my 'infidelity' as you call it. You could've got one or all of us killed if someone found out, or needed to know what you were, *who* you were. It's life or death stuff. So who is it? I know you didn't pay for that rent-a-jetliner outa your pocket. So convenient! 'We have a hijacked airplane and two dozen troops at our disposal 'cuz we're such good fiddlepickers.' Horsecrap and bullshit. Who is it?"

"I work part-time for the NSA. As I said, they use my services sometimes when I go abroad."

"The N-bloody Suckbutt Assholes, eh? Isn't that just lovely."

"So now you know. It was strongly suggested to me I tell no one, because the more people who know, the less chance I have of being covert. Now Mole will know because you'll tell him."

"I'm sure he already knows. He just keeps his trap shut, unlike me who wanted to know a little more about the woman I sometimes sleep with." Rico regretted that as soon as he said it, because he knew what was coming. And it did.

"I'm just the other woman you sometimes sleep with, you mean. You have not denied sleeping with Roxy. Did you?"

"Since we're not keeping secrets this morning, yes, we did sleep together. Going into Mexico. In El Paso. She came on to me and I never knew you were friends. If I'd known, it would never have happened. But it did. I'm sorry."

"But it did," Sally said, "and you're sorry. Was she good? Tight? A better lover than I am? Did she blow you?"

"Oh come on! Yes, we had a night together there, but we cut it off when we found out you two knew each other."

"So you admit to your infidelity, you worthless fucking bastard."

"Goddamn it Sally, it's over between Roxy and me," Rico lied.

"I doubt it, Rico. What happened in Caracas? Eh? Both of you looked well-fucked when I showed up, her on the back of your motorbike."

"We were running for our lives, which might have made us look...er, happy and relaxed, when we finally got away. You looked pretty smooth your own self after we got you and Cassie out of that alley. For Christ's sake, Sally, you're my girlfriend, not Roxy. Can we please move past this now we've admitted our deep, dark secrets to each other?"

"Your ex-girlfriend, Mr. Morgan. You can go fuck Roxy all you want because you and I are through. You think it's a crime I kept my NSA involvement from you, yet you think it's okay to bone my friend all day and night because you don't know she's my friend. I bet you diddled Roxy in Mexico, too, after I sent her down there to watch your sorry ass."

Rico said nothing. He knew if he spoke it would be to drive the wedge between them even deeper. He didn't bother to say good night, and walked out to his car and drove from Sally's house to his own place. His cats greeted him, and soon all was quiet in the Idaho mountains.

And so Sally left. She packed a few bags and flew to London. Sally had friends there, including a man who trained protection and guard animals, including the great black leopard that saved her butt on a lonely road the last time she was in

England. That man was Zak Dragon, whom Sally admired. Rico knew she did. Rico assumed she was there having mad sex with Zak while feeding Rico's broken heart to the hungry leopard. Worse, he knew it was all his own damn fault.

Rico stayed in the park in Atlanta the entire afternoon. On the way back to his hotel room he bought himself a bottle of Famous Grouse and a big bottle of Schweppes soda water and took them to his room. He ordered a simple dinner of a hamburger, fries, and salad through room service, ate alone, drank alone, and felt even worse than he had that morning.

"So," Rico thought, "here I am in Atlanta. Sally's in England. Mole's in Spain with Cassie. Roxy's... who knows where. I don't know a soul in this town and I can't call anyone back home. All the people I care about are off doing their own things, leaving me here to rot." The Scotch was working on Rico's mood and not really improving it. "Who gives a crap about Rico Morgan right now? No one, is the safe guess. So what do I do now to solve this computer-based problem and the murder of the man who hired me?"

The sun sank in the west, behind Rico as he gazed east out the window toward the distant unseen ocean. The shadows lengthened as he watched, the city sank into darkness with lights appearing now here, now there, and now everywhere, and still he stood staring out toward the east.

CHAPTER 6
Thinking

In the morning Rico took an aspirin and some vitamin B12 and ordered coffee. He was on his second cup of coffee when it hit him.

"Something's wrong." Rico spoke out loud to himself. "There's no reason this guy Farchex in Morocco should blatantly kill that man, Harumfer, who was only about to hire me – hadn't done so yet – to find out what's wrong with their robotics computers. Doesn't matter how much of a grudge he might still hold, twenty years later. So far as we know, Farchex doesn't hold a grudge against the man he killed, either. Could there be another reason for Harumfer's death? The only thing comes to mind is to prevent him from hiring me. But that didn't work. I got hired."

Rico continued talking to himself. "Farchex can't be stupid, not if he could get to where he is today, the head of a big company. If Farchex was actually responsible for the laptop all he's done by killing this guy is to shine a light onto himself. If he has half a brain he'd never do that. Gotta think about that. All last night's booze isn't helping, but something in the hooch might have opened my eyes up to this."

Rico paced the hotel room, uncertain as to what to do next and where to go. This went on for another cup of coffee, and then he picked up the hotel courtesy phone and ordered a decent breakfast. Bacon, eggs, toast, another pot of coffee, some ham, orange juice, bananas, the works. In short order everything he could think of that he might want to eat, first thing in the morning, came in the door of his room. He sat and ate, and ate and thought, and ate some more for several hours, as his brain slowly came back to him and the ghosts of the Scotch wore off.

"I need to talk with someone," Rico thought. "Maybe Yeats. Or I can talk to myself a while and see where it goes. I'm gonna try that."

Rico looked into the mirror and started talking out loud. "What do I know for sure? The Luftin-Borlew company is getting diddled by bad chips. This seems to point to an outside source that wants to ruin the company. Only two companies make the diddly, random-activity chips, the Farchex company in Casablanca, called Fortune Technologies, and the other company in Illinois, Fission Chips. I suspect the new and relatively small Illinois company doesn't make suitable chips for robotics machinery...though they do in fact make bogus ones for computer games. I think they're pretty much out of the loop. That leaves the Casablanca outfit, the owner of which is supposed to have a grudge against Boris Luftin and company.

"That Casablanca outfit is most likely getting its bogus, random-diddling chips inserted into the serious robotics computers of Luftin-Borlew. That means Luftin-Borlew must be buying some of their good chips, or computers with them installed, from the Casablanca company. Luftin said they came from some random clearing house. Some of the chips – most of them – work perfectly, but some have the code to go haywire after so many cycles. One simple solution for L-B would be to replace all the chips in all their computers with good new ones, but Luftin indicated the scale of that makes it both very expensive and very time-consuming. The buyers and users won't go for that, so that's out.

"Can anyone tell good from bad chips? If so, the bad ones could be replaced, but with thousands of units in service and the mandatory shut-down and reprogramming, retesting, and so forth after chip replacement, that's not viable either.

"What's the effect of the bogus chips so far? Other than a few wounded workmen and spoiled products, what do we have? A significant drop in sales, as the CEO, Harumfer, told me. Now he's dead. The CEO of the company is dead, apparently by his own laptop computer. That's been established. Where did that killer computer come from? I was told by Luftin that it came from a company that received significant donations from the Luftin-Borlew company. I need to check that. Or have Yeats check that. What else?

"Luftin sez he recalls Farchex had a grudge against him from back in college. The fight actually got him his wife. How about I talk with her and see what she remembers, to get some idea of how bad this grudge could be. She used to know and even date Farchex, the suspected bad guy. And I need to talk with her without her husband being there. It's time I started being the detective they pay me to be."

Rico got up and paced the room, letting the wheels and gears in his head churn a bit in the fresh 'oil' he'd just poured in there.

"For that matter, what's the point of killing everyone who got one of the gifted laptops? Who are the other recipients anyway? I need to know that. But if Luftin and the other laptop recipients all die, what does that do for this fat guy in Morocco?

This big company of Luftin-Borlew won't die just because of the death of some key personnel.

"Man, I just don't see what's going on here. All that's obvious is the L-B company is losing sales to its competitor in Casablanca. So if I follow the money it seems to take me to Morocco. Shit!"

Rico paced more and finally concluded his self-examination with one simple question. "Rico, you dunce, ask yourself, 'Who benefits from the death of Harumfer, the CEO?' I can maybe find that out from the Atlanta PD with a phone call."

Taking the cue from his own rambling, Rico called the Atlanta Police Department and asked to speak with the head of the investigation into the death of Herbert Harumfer. He was connected to Inspector Ralf Raktum. Rico asked him, "Inspector Raktum, I'd like to find out who benefited from the death of Mr. Harumfer. He was apparently not married...."

Ralf interrupted Rico. "No, Mr. Morgan, he *was* still married. He and his wife separated a little over a year ago but never filed for divorce. He owned some fifteen percent of the available stock in the company, and had a vote on the board of directors. His personal fortune amounted to quite a few millions of dollars, the exact amount not yet determined, but perhaps more than twenty million. His wife is the main beneficiary in his death."

"Aha!" Rico paused for a few seconds while he digested this bit of news. "So where is his wife?"

"She lives just outside of Atlanta."

"Can you give me her name and address?"

"Sure. Just a second. Okay, she's Virginia, or Ginny, last name still Harumfer. I have her address...." The Inspector gave it and Rico wrote it down.

"Well, thank you for your information, Inspector. I may need to talk with you again. I hope I won't make a pest of myself."

"No trouble, Mr. Morgan. Call me anytime."

Rico paced his room again.

Finally he phoned I. Yeats Prunzalot at Boise Control. "Yeats, I need you to look into the business affairs of this company, Luftin-Borlew Industries, to find out how well they are actually doing. I know they're suffering currently from loss of sales because of faulty chips and damage to the things the robotics are building, but what about before that? Please find out, maybe with the help of Eileen and the other members of Control, what has been going on with this company for, say, the preceding three to five years."

"Ah, Mr. Morgan, I can do that for you. I have already looked to some extent and things have not been entirely rosy for this company. In fact eighteen months ago they were considering filing for bankruptcy. That is by rumor, not by fact, by the way. I will have the facts verified by Eileen this afternoon."

"Bankruptcy? That would explain a few things. Please keep digging and let me know what you find."

"Are you staying in Atlanta now, kind sir?"

"Yes, Yeats, I'll be here for a while yet. I have to talk with some people that might be involved with both the death of the CEO, Harumfer, and some odd business dealings that have yet to see the light of day."

"Very good, sir. I'll be in touch shortly."

Early the next day Rico drove to the outskirts of Atlanta to the address of Harumfer's estranged wife Virginia. Rico, wearing a sports jacket, black shirt and black jeans knocked on the door of the up-neighborhood home, set back thirty yards from the street. This was, Rico noticed, a posh neighborhood.

After a long wait the door opened. Virginia Harumfer was tall, wore a plain blue dress, low shoes, and had her nearly black hair in a bun. Her eyes were blue and blazing in a near-chalk white face. Her expression was, Rico thought, that of a startled deer. She was a good deal younger than Rico expected, and quite attractive.

"Yes, may I help you?" she said.

"Are you Mrs. Virginia Harumfer?"

"Yes, but I'm not buying anything today."

"Good, because I'm not selling anything. I'm Rico Morgan and I'm looking into the death of your estranged husband, Herbert. Might I come in?"

Long pause. "I suppose so, but I don't know how I can help you. Are you with the police?"

"No, ma'am, I'm an independent investigator. I've been hired by Luftin-Borlew to determine the source of computer problems within the company as well as find out who killed your husband."

"Well, then, come on in." Mrs. Harumfer led Rico to the back of the house where a French door looked out onto a well-kept patio. Beyond that was a large fenced grassy area with flowers here and there. "Please be seated, Mr. Morgan Would you like tea?"

"No thank you, ma'am."

"Please call me Ginny. Now, what do you think I can tell you about Herbert's death or the problems at the company?"

"Anything at all might be useful, er, Ginny. Did Herbert have any enemies? Anyone who would have liked to see him fly off the face of the earth? Any problems that you know of?"

"Herbert – I called him Herbie – was gregarious, lots of friends, no enemies that I knew of. He was the sort of guy who'd bring home a lost puppy and make sure to get it back to the place it belonged. He'd go out of his way to help...anyone. So no, I can't imagine why anyone would want him dead."

"How did he get along with the other top people at Luftin-Borlew? Any fireworks?

"None that I know of. He was close with Boris – Mr. Luftin, the owner. I don't recall Herbie ever talking about the other top officers of the company."

"Were you still close with Herbert? Pardon my asking, but it might help shed some light on this."

"No. We've been separated a long time now. I don't know why we haven't formally divorced. I guess we, neither of us, found time to do it."

"Well, it seems like it was ultimately very good for you that you did not divorce, because now it looks like you inherit his stock and his bank account, which I understand is quite large."

"Yes, I guess I do, but I don't need the money and I'd just sell the stock. Or hold it if my banker or broker says it's a good idea. Frankly, Mr. Morgan, except for some sadness at the loss of a friend, I was not all that greatly affected by the death of my estranged husband. As I said, we were no longer close. We had no children, and I wasn't close with any of his siblings. I hadn't spoken with him in over six months. At least."

"What siblings did he have?"

"He had a brother and a sister. They live on the west coast, so they were never here. We were married only six years, seven including the separation, so I didn't have much chance to get to know his family. He wasn't close with them. That's why his will left everything to me. I don't believe he changed it since we separated."

Rico glanced at some notes he'd put together that morning. "About the company's problems with their computers. Have you heard, or do you know anything at all about that?"

"No. I have no connections with the company at all. I know one or two of the people who work there, but we never talk about the company."

Rico looked out the back window of the house. A rabbit crossed the grass at the far end of the fenced yard, heading for a row of flowers and the surrounding brush. It disappeared.

Rico stood up. "Thank you for your time, Mrs. Harumfer. Ginny. I may call on you again, if that would not be an intrusion."

"That would be fine, Mr. Morgan. I wish you good luck in your investigations." Ginny stood to show Rico out.

As Rico turned to follow Ginny, his eye passed over and then returned to a photo on the nearby mantel. It was of Ginny and a man who was not Herbie. Rico stared hard at the photo for a second and then he followed Ginny Harumfer out.

Rico's next stop was at the house of Boris Luftin. Rico wanted to speak to Luftin's wife, Becky, alone. He'd phoned first, to make sure Boris was not at home, and when Becky confirmed that, Rico asked if he could meet with her. She gave him her address and directions, and it was not an hour after Rico left Ginny Harumfer that he was ensconced in the vast and ancient home of Boris Luftin, talking with Becky Luftin.

She was, Rico thought, showing mid-age spread with a slightly bulging stomach and heavy thighs that showed through the tight jeans she wore. She also had on a plain gray sweatshirt with no logo, and her brown hair hung loosely to her shoulders. Here and there it was flecked with gray, and Becky made no effort to hide it. She appeared to Rico to be somewhat tired, or else had a perpetually tired expression on her pleasant, smiling face. She met with Rico in the house library.

Rico decided to cut to the chase, rather than make small talk about the weather and whatnot. "Mrs. Luftin, your husband told me the story of how you met. This was back in college, right? Can you go through that for me, please? Give me your side of the story?"

"Oh, my. I think so. That was a long time ago." She considered her response a minute. "We met, got together really, one night at a bar, and it was kinda strange. I was a junior and he was a senior. I knew Boris slightly before that night, but I was dating another fellow so never had anything to do with Boris before then, before that night"

"Can you recall any of the details of that night?" Rico asked.

"As best I recall, I went into this popular off-campus bar with a fellow I'd been dating...."

Rico interrupted. "What was his name?"

"August Farchex. I called him Augie. Anyway, we went into this bar and he said 'Hi' to Boris, and we sat to get a drink."

Rico's head came up from his notes, and he stared hard at Becky but did not interrupt her.

"Shortly after, Boris came over to our table and sat down and started to talk with Augie. Kind of oddly, he kept staring at me. I wondered what was up. These guys knew each other from some years back but were not, at that time, close friends. Sort of acquaintances on speaking terms."

Rico could not keep quiet any longer. "Hold it. You're telling me Boris and August Farchex knew each other?"

"Yes, but as I said, they were not close friends. Anyway, after a few minutes Boris started chatting me up. I think he'd had a few too many. I started answering him and Augie started to get somewhat upset. As I said, Augie and I were sort of dating, not all that exclusively, and we were never lovers. We'd known each other for a month or so. It was clear that Boris wanted to get seriously together with me and Augie didn't much care for that. In fact, he asked Boris to cut it out, and Boris said, 'Make me!' Augie stood up and Boris did too, and without any foreplay Boris smacked Augie on the face, slapped him sort of, grabbed him, twisted his arm, and walked Augie outside. He came back and we chatted a while, and then left together. We hit it off that night and we've been together ever since."

Rico sat and stared at Becky and then looked out the window for a few minutes, saying nothing. Finally he said, "So that's it? Boris and August were acquaintances, and Boris wanted to, er, steal you from him? August never took a swing at Boris?"

"Oh hell, no! August was a sort of thick, soft guy with a great mind. He'd never take a swing at anyone."

"What happened when Boris came back into the bar from throwing August out?"

"We sat and talked, and then left the bar together, as I said."

"Did anyone in the bar mention the, er, fight at all? Cheer Boris, for instance?"

"No, not that I recall. Boris had been pretty fit a few years before I knew him, but was almost as soft as Augie at the time. I've often wondered why Augie didn't come back in and challenge Boris to try to get me back. It was kind of strange, but we made it work. Actually I was not that close to Augie, and as I said we were like friends, never lovers. I heard later Augie quit school because of this, and went to another college."

Rico sat and digested this for a while, sipping his tea. He glanced at the books on the library shelves and saw a lot of technical books, and also quite a few novels, and some of the filler-type books put in fake libraries of tract homes on the real-estate market to try to make the prospective new owner look like an intellectual. Several of the shelves were filled with decorations like small bronze statues, fancy glassware, and one or two vases with fake flowers in them. A couple of golf trophies were on one bookshelf prominently.

"Mrs. Luftin, do you have any children?"

"No. We could not have them – Boris's problem, not mine – and didn't care to adopt. We have a dog and two cats and that's it for our 'kids.' "

"Excuse me for asking, but this is a murder investigation. How do you and Boris get along these days? Any problems?"

"We don't spend a lot of time together. Boris goes off occasionally on his yacht. He's got a big sailboat and takes it off somewhere down the coast, sometimes for a week. I don't care for sailing so I let him go and do his thing."

"He goes alone? That sounds like a big chore, one man handling a big sailboat."

"He takes one or two of the guys from the company with him. They go camping on one of the islands down the way, or just anchor and sleep on the boat. It's got a built-in kitchen, galley he calls it, and it can sleep four easily."

"So you and he have lots of time alone, it would seem. Do you have any hobbies that keep you active when he's gone?"

"Yes. I'm an avid golfer, and I welcome his time away, because he doesn't play and I have a hard time getting out onto the links when he's around here. There's too much to do, go to parties and the like, when we're both here together. I don't much care for that kind of life. So we have our separate things and we're both glad of it."

"Mrs. Luftin, I thank you most wholeheartedly for your time. You've opened my eyes up, though I'm not exactly sure right now what it is I'm seeing, but I think you may have helped me look in a different direction from where I've been looking."

"Mr. Morgan, that sounds a bit odd, but if it makes sense to you, then that's good. I liked Herbie Harumfer, and I'd sure like to see his killer found and punished."

Rico left, drove his rental car back to his hotel, went to his room, poured himself a large Scotch and soda, and stared out the window some more.

CHAPTER 7
Manny

Rico ate a resounding early dinner at a nearby restaurant. Then he walked the streets of Atlanta in the late afternoon and thought to himself what exactly he now knew. Talking to himself, he said, "It would appear there's some intrigue going on. Luftin and his wife are no longer close. Harumfer's wife – what's her name? Ginny – doesn't miss her husband at all. *They* were never close, it appears. So who *is* close? From the photo on the mantle at Harumfer's, there's a connection between Ginny Harumfer and Boris Luftin, because that was *his* mug in the photo, not her dead husband. She seems to have got over him way too soon."

Rico walked on. His brain was not yet fully clear from the fog of the night-before-last's binge. "I need a workout, like at a gym," he said to himself. "Sweating out the poisons might help me think better." He suddenly remembered he had a friend in this city who used to run a gym. "If I can remember the guy's name, maybe he still runs the gym and I can go there and have a workout. That'd do me some good. What was that guy called?

That's it! Arkald! Manny Arkald runs a gym in Atlanta. Now, where is it, if it still exists?"

Rico walked into a nearby bar and asked to see a phone book. The barkeep fished around and pulled one out, a huge and mangled old tome. "Not many people come in here to use a phone book these days, mister," said the barkeep with a frown. "They usually come in here and buy a drink."

"Okay, pilgrim," remarked Rico. "See if you can make me a Scotch on the rocks. Decent Scotch, please. None of that Islay stuff."

"How decent?"

Rico put a ten-dollar bill on the bar and replied, "About that decent, and keep the change."

The bartender came back with a glass of some kind of hooch on ice, sat it down in front of Rico and asked, "How's Glenfiddich Twelve?"

"Superb. Thanks." Rico took his drink and the battered old phone book to a table. After rummaging through the yellow pages he found it. 'Manny's Gym.' He took the book back to the bar. "Do you know where Manny's Gym is located?"

"Sure. It's right around the corner. A block north and almost a block west of here. Want another drink?"

"No, thanks." Rico headed out again into the fast-coming evening. A short walk brought Rico to the gym. The entrance was unassuming and looked old though well kept, with a neon sign proclaiming the name and ownership on a darkened glass front. Rico walked in.

"Hi, can I help you?" The man behind the counter was indeed Manny Arkald. He was in his early fifties. Rico had last seen him nearly a decade ago when he was in Atlanta on business, and had met Manny in the course of that work. Manny's daughter had been part of the problem, which Rico managed to sort out. She'd been accused of being a drug dealer in high school but had been cleared by a short investigation by Rico and the Boise Control personnel. Rico did not expect Manny to recognize him. He was wrong.

"Manny..." was all Rico could say before Manny's face lit up like a light bulb turned on behind his dark eyes.

"Rico Morgan! Son of a gun, what in heck are you doing in Atlanta? I thought I'd never see you again!"

"Manny, how'd you recognize me? It's been nearly ten years since you last saw me."

"Hell, old buddy, not that many people are all that ugly. You stick your face in here and I'll either get frightened or recognize you right off."

"Ah, yes, the discerning eye," said Rico. Manny, you old wart, I need your help."

"Well, Mr. Ricardo, judging from your decrepit physique I doubt I can help you. But I'll be glad to take your money and try!"

"Once a crook always a crook, eh? Say, how's Mandy?" Mandy was the girl formerly accused of drug dealing.

"She's married, moved to Florida, has a kid, and is doing very well. She has her own business at home. Her husband's a truck driver, young fellow doing well too, out on the road a lot but not too much. Mandy's pretty happy, all things said. How have you been? Any new or good cases in your hat?"

"I've been fine. Been shot at a time or two over the years, but they missed. Actually, Manny, a case brought me to Atlanta. For the Luftin-Borlew company."

"Oh, man, I heard they're going down."

"The hell you say! What do you know about that?"

"They were in the dumps a couple years ago, or heading for it. Then they got good again but now I hear their CEO got whacked. Oh! So that's why you're here?"

"Yep. That and some odd stuff with their computers here and there. They sell to Tesla, Amazon and a few other big names, but their robotics are apparently being jammed or hacked, which doesn't do the company any good at all. Mostly it's the murder, which seems to be related to the computer problem. The CEO was killed by his own computer."

"See! See! That's why I hate the damned things. Hafta have one of course, for the biz here, but I let someone else take care of it. My brother-in-law, actually. But wait a minute. You said I could help you. Do I get to carry a gun? Go on stakeout? What gives?"

"Manny, I need a good workout. I'm trying to think through a problem and its many turns and twists. I got plastered a couple days ago and haven't had a clean, clear thought since then. I wanna sweat it out. What can you do for me? Weights? Treadmill? Hot sex with some bimbo in the back room?"

"Nuts! Here I thought I was going out on a case with a distinguished detective. Now all I gotta do is call up some bimbo. But I ain't gonna do that, pilgrim. I think you need the medicine ball. Or the weights. I got lots of weights that'll make you sweat. You ever pound the bag?"

"No. If it comes to that I try to shoot first and pound, or punch, later. Sometimes I use a club. Weights might be okay. How about a treadmill?"

"Too slow. You'll wear yourself out before you get a good sweat goin'. I'll set you up in the back room with one of my machines. Pull it or push it or row it to a good weight and in half an hour you'll be a new man. Unless you got a heart condition, in which case you'll be a dead man. Whadda ya say?"

"Weights it is."

Manny set Rico up on one of the adjustable exercise machines, and Rico started huffing and puffing his way back to solid sobriety. When he was done, about half an hour later, Manny joined him and said, "Rico, I've got something to show you. You go hiking much?"

"Once in a while, whenever I can."

"You carry a walking stick?"

"Yes, again whenever I can. If I don't have one I look for a suitable dead stick and use that on my hikes."

"I've got just the thing for you, Mr. Morgan, private eye. Come with me."

Manny led Rico to the back of the gym, reached into a small closet and pulled out what looked like a shaft of wood, about six feet long and just under an inch in diameter. He handed it to Rico.

"What's this? A walking stick?"

"It's a Rootie Stick. Fling it at the wall like a spear."

"The concrete-block wall?"

"No, that wood part over there."

Rico tossed the walking stick gently at the wall. It struck on its end, bounced off and fell the to the floor.

"Now throw it like you mean it," said Manny. "Throw it hard!"

Rico retrieved the walking stick, walked back to stand next to Manny, turned and flung the stick hard at the wall, like he wanted it to penetrate ten bad guys all standing in a row, one behind the other.

As the walking stick left Rico's hand there was a loud *click*, and the forward halves of the Rootie Stick opened abruptly and folded back along the shaft, exposing a foot of the stick's steel core as the stick flew to the wall. The steel core was a hardened rod with a triangular-sharpened point. The point struck the wall, penetrated six inches into the wood paneling, and stuck there, trembling.

"What the heck?" Rico was amazed.

"Yep," said Manny, "when you mean business the stick takes over, inertia opens the shields which spring back, assisted by the wind from high-speed travel, and your 'walking stick' becomes a deadly weapon."

"That's amazing!" Rico was truly impressed. "Can you open the front without throwing it?"

"Yes," replied Manny as he pulled the stick out of the wall. "One way is you can bang the other end on the ground. Another way is to use this grip-like thing at the back. Give it a twist and the covers spring open to expose the point." He shut the forward covers, twisted the handle and the covers sprung open again. Manny closed the covers again, put one end of the stick on the ground, put his foot halfway up the shaft and pulled on the handle. The stick bent slightly and sprung back straight when he took his foot off.

"What the hell!?" Rico was amazed. "How come it didn't crack? It looks like ash on the outside."

"It ain't ash, Rico, it's a composite of flexible epoxy developed by West Systems. It covers a matrix of titanium wire, kind of like screening, which holds the covering together and also protects the steel core. It's finished to look like ash." He handed the stick to Rico. "The core is spring steel so it'll give when you try to break it. And you can use it like a Japanese or Chinese fighting stick, if you know that sort of routine."

Rico examined the stick, flexed it across his knee, hefted it, twirled it, and smiled.

Manny took back the stick, walked to a big, hanging punching bag and swung the stick in a ninja-like manner, striking the bag resoundingly a few times. Then in the middle of his routine he clicked open the front covers and presented the point to the bag.

"I don't want to stick my punching bag. They cost too much. But the sides of the point are sharpened, so you can do some cutting with it if you need to." He closed the point covers, handed the stick back to Rico, and said, "Whatta ya think? Can you use something like this?"

"Hell yes! I need one of these! In fact I can use several. Can you get 'em for me?"

"Not right away. I have that one and one more, with more being manufactured as we speak. They'll retail for three hundred bucks, but I'll give you that one, or one just like it, for a hundred."

"Sold! Roofy stick? Is that what you called it?"

"Rootie. Like Rootie-Kazooty. Only without the dumb hat and the kazoo."

"Rootie stick. Okay! So what do I owe you for the workout?"

"On the house. Only, next time you come in here I'm gonna have to go out on patrol, or stakeout, or something exciting with you. None of this 'Gee, I need a workout' crap!"

"Okay, Manny, I promise you'll go out on the streets with me next time I come by here. Can you ship the stick to my Idaho home? Good, here's the address."

Rico took his leave, waved down a cab, and was soon back in his hotel room.

"It's time to take action," said Rico to himself the next morning, which was a Friday. "I've gotta see Boris Luftin again. See about that boat. See if I can weasel out of him the fact that he's cheating on his wife. That seems to be the case. Maybe I better talk to Yeats and see if he's got any news about Boris's company...before I go off the deep end."

Rico phoned I. Yeats Prunzalot in Boise. A recorded message told the caller Yeats was in Mexico with his father and would be gone for several days.

"Crap! If he didn't bother to tell me he was leaving Boise it must be something serious. And Mexico indicates Yeats's father wants the best medical staff and treatment he can find. Therefore it must be serious. Maybe Kikkie knows something."

Rico phoned Kikkan DaKrotch in Boise on her cell phone and when she answered the call Rico said, "Kikkie, what gives with Yeats? Is his father sick?"

"Rico! I've been trying to reach you. Your hotel in Atlanta said they'd relay a message to you, but obviously they haven't. Yeats's father Sukkan had a mini-stroke and before it got any worse he flew to Mexico City, and is now undergoing some tests there. Yeats is with him."

"The bleedin' hotel here didn't say anything at all to me, Kikkie. But I've been out on the town a lot. Hold on. Someone's beating on my door."

Rico opened the door to find a man in a suit holding a message on a platter for him. Rico tipped the man and opened the note, which said just what Kikkie had said. He picked up the phone again.

"Kikkie, I just got notice of your calls. The hotel finally delivered the messages. Do you know any more about Sukkan's condition?"

"He's all right from what Yeats said. Yeats thinks his dad will fly back in a few days and Yeats will then return to Boise. Yeats left some notes for you."

"What'd he find out about Luftin-Borlew? Anything?"

"Yes, that's what most of this is about. I'm at his house, in the office. Lemme see.... Okay, here's the latest on the company. Two years ago the company filed a brief for bankruptcy, but cancelled within a week. There was apparently some funds run into the company from an unnamed source that permitted the company to continue. The funds came from out of the country, by the way."

"From where, exactly?"

Kikkie said nothing for a while and then, "From Portugal, it seems, from these notes here. I'll have to double check, or have Yeats do so when he gets back."

"Portugal. Okay," said Rico. "What else?"

"Here's a note that says...I'll read it. 'Farchex and his company – Fortune Technologies – may not be the source of the odd chips that seem to be causing the computer problems. Please try to obtain one of the faulty chips directly from one of the faulty robotics machines and send it to me.' That's all it says."

Rico hung on the phone for a minute, mumbling. Finally he spoke up. "Kikkie, there's a good chance of some strange things going on here among the company higher-ups. I can't just ask the man for one of the faulty chips because he may be involved. I'll need to go to one of the companies that's been affected by this problem and extract the chip directly, and do it without the knowledge of anyone at Luftin-Borlew. Who were the companies involved? I recall one was Amazon."

"Uh, yes, and here's another note from Yeats' board. This one was tacked near the top, explaining...this and that. Hold on a sec." Kikkan set down the phone. Rico could hear her walk to the other side of the room, and then heard her return. "You might try Tesla, in Fremont, California, and another one is...."

"Stop right there. I'll go talk with Elon Baby, see if he can dig one out for me."

"Elon Baby?"

"That's what I call him behind his back. He's a great guy. I met him when a friend of mine in Salmon bought one of his cars and Elon personally delivered it. He did that sort of thing a year or so ago, back when he was dating Claire. They had some great ideas together. Dunno if those two are still on, though I heard she's pregnant with his kid, so I guess they are. But I think I can make Elon remember me. I'll let you know. Might need y'all to set up a plane ticket to Fremont. Thanks for your help."

Yeats Prunzalot, head of Rico's Boise Control unit, returned to Boise from Mexico the day after Rico spoke with Kikkan. Yeats set Rico up for a visit with Tesla in Fremont, got Rico's ticket arranged, and gave all the necessary information to Rico on the phone. Rico asked about Yeats' dad. "Yes, my father is now fine. He is back now at Yale, and appears to be in good health. The Mexican doctors determined it was indeed not a mini-stroke, but a combination of the low blood sugar and the migraine. There was actually nothing to worry about, you see, despite his advanced age and sometimes acid disposition. Thank you, Mr. Morgan, for asking. My father sends his kindest regards to you."

"Yeats, I'm mighty glad to hear that. Please let Sukkan know I'm happy he's well. As to his acid disposition, I recommend baking soda in water, taken as often as needed. That, and Scotch on the rocks also taken as often as needed...or even when not needed."

CHAPTER 8
Elon Baby

Two days later Rico left Atlanta on a red-eye to LAX, got a shuttle flight to San Francisco and rented a car to drive to the Tesla plant in Fremont. Yeats had set up an interview with one of the Tesla people named Palante who dealt closely with the computers.

Before he left Atlanta he told his plans to Yeats. "Yeats, in case anyone wonders where I am, after I see the Tesla plant and get the samples or photos of the problem that you need I plan to drive the coastal route, the old Highway One, back to LA. A photographer friend of mine named Danny told me it's well worth doing. He and his wife drove it recently and raved about it, so I've gotta make that drive while I'm out in California. I may never go back there. In fact, if all goes well I will *never* go back to the land of lefties, fruits and nuts, but I might as well do something enjoyable while I'm there. I plan to take my time, see the sights, sleep in Santa Barbara or Ventura, and then head to LAX the next day for my flight to Missoula. If you need me, I won't be available." Rico hated cell phones and didn't carry one unless it was desperately needed and vital to his operation of the moment. "I sure as heck won't need a cell phone along the California coast. At least I hope I don't!"

Yeats replied, "That is very good, Mr. Morgan. If I need to reach you I will contact the California Highway Patrol directly and then they can search for your body in the ocean. Or perhaps I could just call the Coast Guard directly, and save some valuable time while you are under water."

"See you soon, my friend. For your information I won't be packin' heat in California. Too many buttheaded rules and excitable cops."

When Rico arrived at the Tesla plant he told the receptionist he was there to meet with Mr. Palante, chief of computer ops for the section of robotics that gave Tesla the problems.

"He will be with you shortly, Mr. Morgan," the receptionist told him. He's been expecting you. How were things in Atlanta?"

"They were foggy, but that only includes my head, not the weather. Other'n that it was rather nice there."

Rico took a chair and in a few minutes K. Terry Palante walked in. He wore a sort of apron over his clothes, and the apron was spotless. "Mr. Rico Morgan? I'm Terry Palante. Please come with me." Terry spoke with a slight Spanish accent.

"I'm sorry to trouble you with this visit, Mr. Palante, but I thought if I'd just phoned a request I could never be sure it would be satisfactorily answered. I needed to come here to be absolutely certain I get the right thing. And I'm no computer expert. So please bear with me on this little quest."

"That is no problem, Mr. Morgan." They walked down a long corridor with many doors and many lanes branching off the main route. "We are also trying hard to get at the solution to the ongoing problems. If you can help in any way it will be of great benefit to us."

"May I ask where you are from, Mr. Palante?"

"Puerto Rico! Just like the great Daddy Yankee, king of Reggaetón!"

"Ramón Ayala. Yes, indeed. I've seen his videos. Great stuff he does. And the Chapkis dancers! They're my favorites."

Terry Palante looked at Rico directly, as they walked down the hall. "I'm quite surprised you have heard of Daddy Yankee. He is not all that well known in the United States...not yet, at any rate."

"Well, Mr. Palante...."

"Please call me Terry."

"Well, Terry, I'm a great fan of a few extremely talented young dancers, all of whom seem to know each other, and to my amazement they all seem to have television and modeling credits in their resumes at sub-teen ages. My mother was a great dancer and it seems to be in my blood to appreciate great dancing. These young people are actually quite stunning to watch, and I know they're all going places with their lives. One of them is Sarah 'Lil' Mini' Phoenix, and when I saw her dance so well in Dallas with Greg Chapkis' group I couldn't help but watch her with Daddy Yankee in Mexico. She's amazing for a young girl, holding her own – and then some – with the best dancers in the business. She, along with Greg Chapkis, made me a fan of Daddy Yankee. I read that his YouTube video was the most popular in the world in 2019. Quite an achievement."

"*¡Claro que sí! Se llama 'Con Calma.'* Oh, sorry, my Spanish slipped out. Nearly two billion hits on that video. Amazing!"

"No problem, *amigo,* my sometimes partner is a former Mexican national and I'm used to his occasional bursts of his native tongue. I understand you perfectly."

"*Pues,* this is my personal lab." Terry stopped and opened a door. "Come in, please."

The sizeable room was cluttered with tables and shelves containing all kinds of electronic test equipment. Some parts of a damaged robotic arm were in the room as well, and Terry led Rico to the table that held the arm.

"This is part of the machine that went bad a few weeks ago." Terry indicated the arm, which had a grasping component at one end and mounting holes at the other end. "This arm was supposed to grab a panel of the car body from a conveyor-like feed line, lift the panel, turn around a hundred-eighty degrees and place and hold the panel against the side of the car body, and then the panel would be fastened with spot welds. When the computer went bad, instead of lifting the panel to the car the arm began beating on the car body with the panel, and this went on until we turned the unit completely off. It destroyed not only the panel but the entire car body as well. As you might expect, this problem shut down the entire assembly line. It was down for over a week until we could get a replacement computer from a different company, and then program it to do what the old setup did. As you might expect, that cost us a lot of money."

"The computer that drove this arm...did it have any other function?"

"No. It did this job only. Then, about a week after the new system was installed and we were once again in production, another one of the robotic tools went haywire. This one controlled a welder in a different stage of the vehicle production. It was programmed to do a simple weld job but when it failed, the weld head went to the wrong position and zapped the panel, so there was no weld at the right spot. That was not as serious as the arm here. We could easily correct that problem, but again we had to replace the computer to make it all work properly.

"Have you looked into the bowels of the computer that drives this arm?"

"Yes, it's right here on the next table. We probed it, did the suggested tests from the extensive repair manual, but came up with nothing. In fact it seems almost right, now. But we can't risk putting it back into production."

"What I'd like to do is take a close look at the main computer chip, the one that drives most of what's happening. Can you show me that?"

"Er...yes, it's plugged into the motherboard under this heat-dispersion shielding. Let me grab a tool here..." Terry fished into a toolbox on the table. "There. The heat sink is outa the way. Lemme wipe that clean. Now you can see the chip."

There was no maker's name visible on the chip.

"I would have expected," said Rico, "to see some sort of identification on the top surface of this chip, under the heat-dispersing grease, or next to it. That is most odd. The only other place for the identification of the maker is on the underside, or maybe around the edge, but no chip maker is gonna force the user to pull the main chip off the board to read the maker's name and ID number from the bottom side. Can you pull off the chip? Actually I'd like to take it with me if that's possible."

"Wait a minute, Mr. Morgan. There appears to be some abrasion on the top of the chip where a number or maker's mark would normally be." Terry grabbed a magnifying glass and peered at the chip. "Yes, it's been defaced. The name and numbers have been scraped or sanded off. None of the original markings are visible. That's odd. Yes, I'll pull the chip and you can take it along. It is no good to us at this time."

"Can we look at the computer that controlled the welder, and also at some good, functioning computers' main chips?"

"The welder's computer is in the corner over there, near the trash can."

A few minutes' work and the main chip in that computer was also found to be without any markings, and showed carefully hidden but still viable signs of it having been defaced like the other one.

Terry spoke. "We can look at a functioning computer in the main assembly room. All of the assembly computers on that line are temporarily stopped. It will be the work of seconds to look at several of their computer hearts."

Twenty minutes later Rico and Terry had looked at half a dozen computer chips, installed in the temporarily shut-down assembly line. Two of them had defaced chips. The other four had the name of Fortune Technologies – the company of August X. Farchex, the gentleman who supposedly had a grudge against Boris Luftin and his robotics company – distinctly imprinted onto their top surfaces.

Rico said, "It appears that Fortune Technologies made all the good chips. Good so far as you and I know, at any rate." Rico pondered this. "The defaced chips appear to be identical to the good ones, other than the lack of a name. I wonder if they left the Fortune factory and were then reprogrammed, and then defaced to mark 'em, somewhere along the line before they got to Luftin-Borlew?"

"That's doubtful, replied Terry. "I understand Luftin-Borlew buys these chips installed by the manufacturer, which apparently is Fortune Technologies. They're installed into Luftin-Borlew's, L-B's, own computer motherboard design. Once the motherboards arrive at the L-B factory the company then assembles each computer in conjunction with its appropriate piece of robotics machinery. Then they program each computer to do its job, whatever is needed, and we here at Tesla get the whole shebang as a completed entity. We usually have to alter the programming setup slightly, fine tune things, but we never mess with the guts of the computer."

Rico thought about that, and said, "The Luftin-Borlew company would have no reason to inspect all the chips, would they? In fact they can't, without removing the heat sink and cooling fins already in place so they can get a good look at what master chip is in the computer. The fins would hide the chips from any inspection."

"I agree," said Terry. "So the damage, the defacing, is done to the chips before they arrive at the L-B plant."

"The reprogramming, or the bogus programming, would be done before they arrive, too. Who touches the chips before they arrive?"

"After they're made and installed in the L-B motherboard, which is done by the chip maker, probably no one. If they're from overseas and coming into the country in quantity there would be importation inspections to make sure they are what it says on the invoices and importation papers, but they'd never dig in to look at the chips. No need."

"I was told by Boris Luftin, the owner of the L-B robotics company, the chips were purchased from an electronics clearing house. That, apparently, is not true. If they're installed in the motherboards by the chip maker, it means the bad chips are coming right out of Fortune Technologies along with the good ones."

"Yep!" Terry agreed.

"So now it's my job to find out when and where the chips, if they're in fact all made by the same company, are being buggered." Rico scratched his head.

"Yep."

Rico took photos of the good and bad chips, packed two good and two bad chips carefully in a box, thanked Terry for his help, made his way back to the lobby and started to leave. On the way out he spotted 'Elon Baby' near a drinking fountain, walked over to him, and as he did Elon recognized Rico, waved, and said "Hi, Rico. What brings you to California?"

Rico said, "Your computer problems bring me here, as a matter of fact."

"Ah," said Elon, "I recall now. You're an investigator. Can you tell me what's going wrong with our stuff?"

"Not yet. I just looked at one of the failed computers, the main chip of which seems to have been tampered with."

"Aha! I told my design team in our last meeting it might be a good idea to start making our own computer chips. I think we might press ahead with that. Er, tampered with? How?"

Unnoticed by Rico or Elon in the Tesla lobby with all its human traffic, a short, dark-complexioned, slightly stocky, bearded man stood not far away from the drinking fountain, and easily overheard the conversation. He fiddled with his pen, then with his handkerchief wiping his glasses, and stayed within earshot as Rico talked with Elon.

"How was it tampered with? The identity of the main control chip's maker was defaced, essentially removed. It was also removed from several chips in computers on your far-right assembly line, which is now temporarily shut down for some reason. We, your man K. Terry Palante and I, examined the chips and found some in that assembly line that had the name defaced on top. I'd bet they'll be some of the ones that fail in the none-too-far future."

"I hope Terry marked them so we can monitor that."

"Yes, he did."

"So what's the next step? I know we can replace those before they fail if that's the real problem here, but what are you doing to find out the story behind 'em?"

"I'm going back to my home in Idaho and have my gang take a long, hard look at what we have. I've got two each of good and bad chips to analyze. I have a suspicion, in fact several, but it takes a better computer person that I to dig as deep into this as is needed."

"And you have such a person in Idaho?"

"Yes indeed. My man I. Yeats Prunzalot is a real whiz with computers and all they can do. On a darker note I also have to look into the murder of the CEO of the company that sold you the robotics. I may have to go back to Atlanta."

"I heard about that. Good luck finding the, er, culprit, and please keep me informed. Here's my card with my direct number on it."

"Thanks. I will. By the way, I like those new futuristic-looking trucks of yours. If I needed one I'd surely have one...after a really good payday, of course!"

"Well, Rico, if you ever do need one let me know, and I'll be sure you get some extra features that might help you in your line of work."

"Bulletproof windows would help."

"Can do!" Elon smiled, shook hands, and Rico took his leave.

As Rico got into his rental car for the drive back to the airport the short, dark, bearded man get into a car at the same time. The man left the parking lot behind Rico's rental, and stayed a quarter mile behind until they got out of sight of the factory. The man removed his false beard and replaced it with a nasty smile.

He followed Rico's car into the turnoff that led to the Pacific Coast Highway, also called Highway One. The short, stout man stayed within sight of Rico's car as they drove south along the beautiful scenic drive. A good number of miles south of Fremont, as they drove into the Big Sur country, the man following Rico made his play.

The highway ran along the edge of a cliff, with a drastic drop-off of several hundred feet to the ocean on the right side. There was no guard rail, a common feature all along that two-lane road, and the shoulder was only a few feet wide along there. On the left side of the road was a cliff going abruptly up, not ten feet from the left edge of the road. The short and stocky man knew of this spot. He knew that at that time of year and time of day there was almost no traffic on the road.

He closed the gap between his car and Rico's rental, and smiled to himself. The dark man noticed that Rico was looking toward the right, admiring the dramatic view, as he approached the critical spot on the road. "Soon he'll be part of the view!" the dark man said to himself. As they approached this preselected spot the dark man accelerated hard into the left lane and came flying up past Rico's car. When he got even with the rental car in the left lane the dark man whipped the steering wheel to the right. His car swerved drastically, driving hard toward the right lane where Rico's rental car was. In a second it would smash into it and knock it off the road. The cliff loomed. The ocean waited.

CHAPTER 9
Roxy

Roxy Roades was in Canberra, New South Wales, Australia, investigating for the U.S. CIA department, of which she was an agent. Roxy had been with the CIA for almost half a dozen years. As a relatively new and youngish member she took whatever the agency threw at her in the way of assignments, and this one took her far from her east-coast-USA home. She was in Australia trying to find out if there was a viable connection between Miles Drapcox, head of the Australian Security Intelligence Organisation, ASIO, in Australia, and George Sorbutt, the financier of so many sinister liberal plots worldwide. She wanted to know if Drapcox was in any way responsible for the horrific wildfires in the extremely dry weather Australia was experiencing. The fires were really bad, and word had it that the worst was yet to come. It was a simple assignment: Gather data on Drapcox in any way possible, which meant clandestinely; interview the man in the guise of an American news magazine for which she had phony credentials; in short, see what he had to hide and what he had to say. Basically Roxy was looking for signs of any collusion, and any dirt on Drapcox.

Roxy Roades was in her late twenties and looked a lot like Emma Roberts, but with long blonde hair instead of brown. Roxy had green eyes and a keen intellect that made her advancement in CIA circles somewhat speedy. She'd helped her sometimes-lover Rico Morgan on dangerous assignments in New Mexico and in Caracas, Venezuela. Now she was in Canberra with another woman from the CIA, Mary Teslin, a fairly new recruit.

Roxy was, "Kind-of breaking you in, in a great way in a great country," as she told Mary. "This is a posh assignment. Gets both of us out of Washington, DC, for a goodly spell. Who knows, we might even find true love down here."

Mary replied, "Or we might get burned in a wildfire."

Mary Teslin was, like Roxy, young, slim, fit and slightly athletic, all necessary requirements for the field work she and Roxy pulled as assignments. Early in her career Mary learned that the soft and overweight agents tended to get desk jobs at Quantico, or here and there in the U.S., generally stationary or sedentary jobs that were necessary but not much fun. So Mary worked out every day, as did Roxy, to stay field-ready. Her dark-red hair was shoulder length, with bangs so it would not get in her green eyes. Like Roxy she wore slacks that permitted action while still letting her look respectable, and stout shoes in which she could run or fight.

"Get burned? Yes, that too," said Roxy. "But there's no need for us to get into the heart of the blazes. We just need to work like blazes to see if we can get some dirt on this guy Drapcox."

"Explain to me again how we're gonna do that."

"We need to get into his office when no one else is there and root through his personal files to see if there's any record of contact or collusion with Sorbutt."

"There won't be anything there," replied Mary Teslin. "I was taught that at Quantico. Or Palm Beach...? Toledo? I was taught that somewhere, at any rate. The obvious evidence is never gonna be where it's supposed to be by any sort of logic. It's a waste of time trying to find it."

"Bingo! You get a grade of A-plus on that one," said Roxy. "Except that we have to make *sure* there's nothing there. The only other place we might find something is in some memo he forgot about and stuck in his 'Out' box by mistake, or used as a book marker on his bedside table, you know, the easy stuff."

"Can I say 'shit'?"

"You are allowed."

"I already said it. So what do we do first?"

"It might be a good idea to find out exactly what he looks like. His photo, which we have, could be a year old and might not do justice to him as he looks today. So, where's he gonna be tonight?"

"Well, from his personnel file we know he likes opera. So he might be at the local opera house for *Carmen*, which opens tonight."

"I think there's an easier way," said Roxy. "He drinks like a fish, and there's a bar not far from his office, and it's near the time for him to leave his office and make tracks to the closest bar. I know, I know, there's no way a high-dollar butthead is going to mingle with street people and the lesser lights of business-town at a local tavern. But this, remember, is Australia. He's going to want to drink with his countrymen. Be seen, look like he cares, get appointed or elected again, that sort of thing. So there's a great chance he'll be at the local bar in half an hour."

"Let's go!"

"You sound like Greg Chapkis."

"What?"

"I'll explain later. *¡Vamonos!*"

"What?"

Roxy grabbed Mary's arm and headed for the hotel-room door.

"Oh. I get it," Mary said. "But who's Greg Chapkis?"

The two CIA women arrived at the bar just down the street from the building that housed the office of Miles Drapcox. They sat at a table with a good view of the room and waited for the hopeful arrival of their target.

"What if he doesn't show?" Mary fidgeted in her seat.

"Then we'll go to plan B," replied Roxy.

"And what is that, precisely?"

"A drive-by shooting."

A man approached their table. He could have been in his late thirties, possibly older. The marks of booze over time made it hard to judge his age. His eyes were shining from too much booze and from the golden chance he thought he had to talk up two attractive women sitting alone in a bar. "Hi, ladies, mind if I join you?"

Roxy answered. "Yes, we do mind. We're waiting for someone. Thanks for asking."

"Crikey, I could just sit here until your friends arrive, eh, mate?"

"Or not. Please go away."

"Righty. Bitch!" The man sulked off.

As he walked away, the bar door opened and in walked Miles Drapcox. Roxy recognized him from the old photo they had. Drapcox was a small man in his mid-fifties with a pot belly barely disguised by his classic three-piece suit. His dark blond, going-to-gray hair was plastered to his head with some sort of grease, which reminded Roxy of an advertising tune her grandmother used to sing. It popped into her head:

Brylcreem, a little dab'l do ya,
Brylcreem, ya look so debonaire.
Brylcreem, the gals'll all pursue ya,
They love to get their fingers in your hair!

There was no way Roxy wanted to get her fingers in that greasy mess, even if she could ignore his short stature and his fat stomach.

"Yuk," she said. Why doesn't someone tell that guy his hair's out of style by seventy years."

"Nice suit, though," said Mary. "Do we need anything more, now that we know what he looks like?"

"No, but we could take a picture of him. Make it look like we're so much in awe of this Aussie bar we want to send a photo home to our friends in the 'States."

They arranged a 'selfie' with the background carefully chosen to include the dapper chief of ASIO. Just as Roxy was about to take the snap the drunk who had approached them earlier stood up and blocked the image of Drapcox. He looked angry as well as even more drunk.

Undaunted, Roxy moved to the side so Drapcox was again clear in the background, and took the snap. The drunken man once again approached the two women.

"Hey, bitch, take my picture!" He staggered close to the women. Several patrons of the bar looked at him and at the two women.

"Shit. He's drawing attention to us. We don't want Drapcox to notice us. Not if we're going to interview him in a few days." Roxy put her cell-phone camera away, being careful to face away from Drapcox who, she noticed, started to turn around, his attention drawn by the noise from the rowdy drunk. She spotted a rest room at the back of the bar and said, "Come on, Mary, he won't follow us into the john."

The two women went there, always keeping their backs to the important man sitting at the bar, now looking their way, now with a sizeable glass of gin in front of him.

Inside the restroom Mary said, "Whenever we leave here Drapcox will look at us. So what do we do?"

"I saw a back door. We can slip out of here one at a time and sneak out that way. Let's wait a bit here, and then you go first. I'll follow in another minute."

After a short wait that seemed to go on forever, Mary left the rest room, turned right toward the rear exit instead of left to the bar, and made for the back door. She got out with no trouble, and found herself in an alley. A short time later she was joined by Roxy, but right behind Roxy came the drunk who wouldn't quit.

"Hey, babes, thought you were waitin' for someone! How about me! We get together, do a little drink, a little dance, a little roll in the hay, ever'body's happy!" He staggered toward them.

When they first saw him he was slightly drunk. Now he was nearly fall-down smashed. Roxy said to Mary, "Take him down. Be gentle! He's so drunk he might hurt himself."

Mary smiled at the drunk and swung her hips as she got closer to him. "What's your name, big fella?" she asked.

"Call me Jimbo, you sexy bimbo! Let's hook it up, darlin'!" He made a grab for her arm. Mary parried his grab, then grabbed his arm and pulled him, now off balance, over her outthrust leg and let him slide down onto the ground, twisting his arm as he fell so he rolled away from her when he hit. He lay there mumbling for a short time. The girls started to walk down the alley away from the drunk. They were maybe thirty feet away when they heard Jimbo behind them, running and stumbling in their direction. Roxy looked over her shoulder and saw the knife. "Watch it!" she shouted to Mary.

Jimbo was foaming at the mouth. Drool ran down his face. He apparently threw up on his shirt when Mary put him on the ground, and that, combined with the shock of finding himself lying on the chilly ground, sobered him slightly, angered him greatly, and also made him that much more disgusting. He came for Mary, his eyes glued on her. Before he got anywhere near Mary, Roxy took a step toward him, jumped into the air, and drove her foot into his face. This dropped drunken Jimbo to the ground. His knife flew out of his hand and clattered onto the pavement of the alley. Roxy picked it up and tossed it into a nearby dumpster. The two agents then proceeded rapidly down the alley and out onto the main street.

They walked away from the bar and crossed the street into a park, and proceeded under the trees until they were out of sight of the bar in which Miles Drapcox sat drinking gin.

“Well, that was fun,” said Mary. “Nice kick. You do that often?”

“Whenever it’s necessary. So what do we do now, Agent? You call it.”

“Let’s make for his office. We have the address, though it’s gonna be hard to get into a secure building…nah, better idea, let's hit his home while he sits there and drinks."

"Good choice. I think we'd have one heck of a hard time getting into his office and bypassing the security of a security agency. I think I can cover his office in my interview in a couple days."

The two women knew the home address of Drapcox, part of their research before they ever left the 'States. They fast-walked to their rental car and drove the short distance to the home of Miles Drapcox.

"That's a modest house for a man in his position," said Roxy. "I guess they don't pay a lot, or else he's more intelligent that we gave him credit for."

"I get it. An intelligent person would know he may not be the head of his department forever. If he bought a grand home how'd he manage to keep it if he were, say, ousted from his position?"

"Yes, Mary, and also the government might not be paying him all that much. Let's get inside."

They drove around the block in the suburban area where Drapcox lived until they got to the opposite side of his block. They got lucky, as there was no house there, just a bunch of trees. They made their way through the trees to his back yard, where there was a simple pole fence.

"Drapcox is single, so there's no chance of our meeting with a wife, but there's always a chance someone else might be in the house for another good reason." Roxy pondered the break-in casually.

"What if we just go up and knock?" asked Mary.

"And if there's someone there? Then what?"

"We could do a drive-by shooting."

"You're gettin' it! Good call, Mary."

They made their way across his back yard. There was no dog, the yard and house were somewhat isolated from other dwellings in the neighborhood, and they were able to get to the back door without being seen or challenged.

Roxy knocked at the back door while Mary peered into as many windows high and low as she could see. No one was about. In the work of a few minutes they were inside. Mary went to the basement, Roxy upstairs to the bedroom area. After fifteen minutes they met on the main floor. There was a library with a busy-looking desk, and the two women made for that as being the likeliest place to find papers and anything else that would implicate Drapcox in any kind of collusion with Sorbutt, or with anyone else who might be involved in the rampant wildfires.

"What's this?" Mary held up what looked like a letter, taken from a stack of papers she hastily scanned on Drapcox's desk in the library.

"What's it say?"

Mary read it. "It's been decoded. The original text is here, but it doesn't make any sense. Dated yesterday. The decoded part reads, 'Dear sir,' ...blah, blah... 'concerning the supplied funds to your field operatives,' ...blah blah... 'we express our sincere hope that the new tellurium refining and production operation has been incapacitated by the wildfires burning near the location of that operation. As soon as the complete destruction of the factory is verified by our people in the field you'll receive the entire remaining contracted compensation. It will come within the month directly from the Portuguese branch of our Casablanca bank, sent to the account number you provided, to which we posted the initial funding.' Signed, 'August X. Farchex.' Address in Casablanca."

"Bring it. Or, on second thought, leave it and get some good photos of it. Let me hold it so you have valid proof we saw it, rather than forged it."

Mary took the pictures and sent them to their headquarters in the U.S.

CHAPTER 10
Tony and Rose

Back in their hotel room the two CIA woman discussed the operation. "That guy Farchex runs a factory in Casablanca, from what headquarters told you," said Mary. "Looks like Sorbutt was not involved with this operation."

"Not with this one," replied Roxy, "but he might have messed with someone else here in Australia. That's not our job. We did what we needed to do, find dirt on Drapcox. Let's go celebrate!"

That night the two women went to a bar to celebrate their successful operation. The bar featured a guitarist playing flamenco music, which the two women, sitting at a table near the guitarist, thought to be unusual.

"Isn't this a bit odd for Australia?" Mary asked.

"What's really odd is the people are actually paying attention to this guy. He's pretty good, too." Roxy smiled at the guitarist.

"I have no idea if he's good or bad," replied Mary. I'm not at all familiar with this kind of music. I expected maybe some bluegrass, or down-home Aussie folk tunes, but never this kind of guitar stuff."

"My friend Rico Morgan plays some of this stuff. Shut up and let me listen."

The guitarist was deep into an *Alegrias* similar to what the legendary Sabicas played, with – as always with flamenco – some personal interpretations by the guitarist.

Mary and Roxy ordered beer and a plate of nachos and relaxed to the sound of the guitar. Soon the piece ended and the guitarist took a break. Roxy waved him over to their table.

"Hi, I'm Roxy and this is Mary. Who are you?"

"I'm Tony Hammer. I could tell you've heard some of this before. I saw you tapping on the table just like we were in *Andalucía,* but *pues,* you need the proper wine for this occasion, not that crappy Australian beer." He signaled a waitress, and asked for a bottle of a particular type of wine. The waitress went for it as the trio continued to talk about music.

"Tony," said Roxy, "I have a friend back in Idaho who plays some of this type of music. He also plays bluegrass, so he's not a purist."

"Heck, I play classic guitar in addition to flamenco. But classic guitar is too slow and too quiet for a bar, especially this bar, because it gets pretty noisy in here later in the night. There's even some guys and gals who come here and dance flamenco once in a while."

"That'd be great to see," said Mary.

The wine arrived and they all had some. Tony lifted his glass and said, "Here's to your flamenco buddy in Idaho. What's his name, by the way?"

"He's Rico Morgan, the private eye."

"No shit!" Tony said. I know him...well, sort of. We've shared an email or two about old flamenco records over the years. Amazing coincidence, eh? And you know him? Let's drink to coincidences, ladies."

Mary took the opportunity to ask about the fires. "Tony, do you know anything about the wildfires burning down some new facility that dealt in refining metalloids? Up north somewhere?"

"Yes, there was a new factory supposed to refine tellurium and maybe some other stuff. The building was located away from the cities to avoid problems with pollution and the general fear of radiation or whatever the people near such a place might be afraid of. But the wildfires took it down last week. I heard it was totally destroyed. I think the Chinese had a major interest in it."

"Chinese?" Roxy asked. "I know they're close, but what sort of hold do they have here in Australia?"

"Heck, the Chinese meddle in politics here, they own lots of farmland, they're trying to get a long-term lease to control the port in Darwin, and they even built an airport in west Australia that's not even legal, so the politicos say. We Aussies don't much like the incursion of Chinese interests into our country. As I said, that new tellurium refinery that was just destroyed was mainly Chinese owned, so not too many of my countrymen are unhappy about it. How'd you hear about it anyway?"

"Ah,...er," Mary stumbled.

Roxy saved the day. "We heard the Tesla company was going to use the stuff in its new cars, you know, the electrical ones. But hey, what's tellurium used for anyway? Does anybody know?"

A man at the next table turned slowly and addressed Roxy. "Excuse me for interrupting, but I overheard your last question. Tellurium is used in the manufacture of computer chips and solar panels. Also used in some obscure way for heating water faster, I believe. Mr. Tesla – you know, Elon himself – is supposedly looking to start making his own chips rather than buy them from questionable sources, and his company is heavily involved in solar-panel promotion. He was a strong investor in this new company. But it's all gone now, more's the pity. Sorry for interrupting." He turned away.

"Ladies, I've gotta get back to my guitar. Any requests?"

Roxy said, "How about some *Granainas*?"

"Can do," said Tony and he went back to his instrument.

The ladies listened awhile, and then Roxy said, "Let's go. I've gotta be fresh for my interview tomorrow with Mr. Drapcox." They waved goodbye to Tony and took their leave.

The next morning Roxy made her way to the office of Miles Drapcox at ten. She had an appointment to interview him – made by her company – at that hour. All was cleared, and she sat down opposite his desk and set up a recorder.

"I hope you don't mind the recorder. My note-taking is perilously slow and if I speed up I can't read what I've written."

"That's all right, Miss Ruxton." She didn't use her own name for the interview, which was supposedly for a U.S. magazine that dealt with international intelligence stories. The CIA figured it would be easy for ASIO to check who she really was, so a phony name with sufficient background was invented just for this interview. Her pseudonym was Rose Ruxton.

"First off," Roxy asked, "what can you tell me about this tellurium-processing plant that was destroyed by the fire. How did it come about, and what was its purpose?"

"Wow. Bad news travels fast. Yes, it was destroyed just a week ago. It was a clever deal. The Tesla company was one of the major financiers for the project. As you know, the U.S. Trump administration set up some new tariffs that would, or could, increase the cost of all trade goods coming out of China and going to the U.S. To avoid those tariffs, some clever Chinese speculators and some world-wide investors decided to set up a factory here in Australia that would refine Chinese mineral ore here and thus be able to sell tellurium to U.S. concerns without the potential increase in price from import tariffs. As you may know, in past years the U.S. produced some, and also bought some of its tellurium from Canada, but China has become the world's largest producer, with some 300 metric tons coming out of there last year. That's many times what any other country produces, and they even have a dedicated tellurium mine in China with something like eleven thousand workers in just one of their production plants. China was smart. They could see the demand coming, got on the ball and produced and developed product for which the demand has skyrocketed in the last few years.

"The cost of tellurium from this Australian plant would have been considerably lower to U.S. buyers than the same product sold directly out of China. Without the tariff the price of tellurium is so much lower than anywhere else in the world that anyone needing tellurium had to go to China for the best deal. But not with the new tariff in place! If the plant here had survived and been viable, China miners would have benefited just as much as they used to, before tariffs. The plant was, essentially, a way for Chinese businesses to avoid the new U.S. tariffs."

"I see. So the destruction of this facility hurts everyone. China, which may lose a percentage of their former export quantity, Australia which may have benefited from a new job source – unless the workers were all Chinese, of course – and U.S. companies, which will have to either buy directly from China at higher prices or find another source."

"That is correct. The worldwide producers of tellurium, which is used for making computer chips and solar panels – both of which the Tesla people use in abundance – are not all that many. The U.S. used to produce it and probably still does, but your country lost a lot of its manufacturing ability, skills, and initiative by sending production of everything overseas so the big companies could make a few more dollars in the short run. Apple has its cell phones made in China for that reason. I wonder if there's anyone in the United States who can put together a complete cell phone, even if they had all the pieces. It's like Detroit, where so many cars used to be built. Now Detroit's a ghost town. The rest of your country is fast becoming that too, and that will continue until the jobs and expertise come back to the U.S. Another thing is that China has lax emission laws which make it possible for them to refine nasty materials when other countries can't do so. Not at the same prices."

"Thank you for the graphic picture of the ongoing economy. You're right about the loss of job skills in the U.S., and no one knows how to fix it – though our President seems to be trying."

Roxy wanted to ask him how much he got paid to make sure the new factory was destroyed. Instead she asked, "How have the wildfires hurt other areas?

"Well," said Miles Drapcox, "the wildlife has suffered greatly. Quite a few people lost their homes, and this has been a terrific burden for all the Australia people. But we will recover. This sort of thing happens here on a regular basis, if you look at the history of our country."

"I read that many of the fires were set. You've caught over a hundred arsonists so far. Can anything be done about that, such as setting an example with some of them through very harsh punishment? And is there any reason the country is so hot and dry? Seems like that is somewhat unusual this year."

Drapcox considered a minute. "The arsonists will be punished to the extent of the law. Unfortunately that doesn't permit the death penalty, nor is the punishment adequate for their transgressions, in my opinion. However, this season is, as I noted, hotter than most in the past, and I'm afraid this will get hotter as the season progresses and we actually get deeply into our summer."

Roxy asked some further questions on intelligence that were on her list to ask, and Mr. Drapcox readily answered them all. Roxy concluded the interview.

"Mr. Drapcox, thank you kindly for your time and openness."

"You're welcome, Miss Ruxton. I hope I've given you all the information you needed."

Roxy again wanted to say, "No, you bastard. Why'd somebody in Casablanca pay you to wreck that new company?" Instead she said, "I think you have. Best wishes to you, and goodbye."

"So, who is this Farchex guy?" Mary asked Roxy back at their hotel. "Why did he want to stop production here of tellurium? What does he have to gain?"

"Money, I'd bet," replied Roxy. "The root of all evil. If he gives a bunch of money to Drapcox here to destroy that new company – and it had to be *lots* of money to sway this so-called intelligence officer – then it stands to reason Farchex will make it all back ten times over."

"If he's in Casablanca, or wherever, just about anywhere outside the U.S.," Mary reasoned, "he doesn't have to pay any kind of tariff to get that mineral out of China directly. So he's cutting in on the other people and companies that use that mineral...what's it called?"

"Tellurium."

"Yes, and he can get it far cheaper than can, say, Tesla, which wants to make its own chips. So that would indicate Farchex makes chips or, what was the other thing?"

"Solar panels. Mary, you're right on target. But what can we, or anyone, do about it?"

"We could expose Drapcox. We have photos of that letter."

"So what if we expose him and he goes to jail?" Roxy paced the room. "Besides, that's not our job. The home office will do that if it benefits them. Count on it. Exposing him doesn't rebuild the factory either."

"But it would tend to keep the factory standing after it's rebuilt. And the insurance companies would be happy because the money to rebuild will come from Australia, not out of the insurance companies' pockets."

"Well, Mary, that's not what we came here to do. I think we've done our job. I wonder where our next journey will take us?"

"Will we stick together?"

"I think so. You're my trainee, so to speak, though not officially. They just wanted to get us out of the home office and let us play spy over here. Who knows, we might get to Paris or London yet."

"Whoopee," Mary said, with no trace of excitement. "Or maybe to Hong Kong. So what do we do for dinner?"

The phone rang. Roxy got it.

"Miss Roades," said 'Control' at CIA. He identified himself with a certain code which Roxy recognized. Control continued. "There are tickets at the Melbourne airport for you and Mary Teslin to travel posthaste to Casablanca."

"Yes!!" exclaimed Roxy under her breath.

"There you will attempt to discover who, and what, is one August Farchex and see why he had Drapcox burn down that facility there in Australia. If you need any more data or supplies let us know and they will be shipped and held in your name at the Oum Palace Hotel and Spa in Casablanca."

"When do we leave?"

"Tomorrow afternoon," replied Control. "It's an overnight flight, and you'll have just about a full day in the air. You'll take a shuttle from Canberra to Melbourne, and then it's twenty-four or twenty-five hours in the air to make the roughly eleven thousand miles to Casablanca."

Roxy thanked him and hung up, beaming. She turned to her companion and said, "Mary, we're going to Casablanca!"

"What?! Wow! Yess!! Er, when?"

"Tomorrow."

"Crap! We don't get to kiss Tony goodbye."

CHAPTER 11
Offroad

Soon after Rico left the Tesla factory he spotted the car trailing him. He'd suspected it might happen, especially in light of the murder of Herbert Harumfer, who'd contacted Rico in the first place.

"Poopie! I know someone doesn't want me looking into these chips. That's why they killed Herbie Harumfer." Rico carried on a conversation with himself in his head. "Hoibie would have been okay if he hadn't sent me the little Howdy Doody robot and asked me to look into it. Whoever planted the bad chips wanted him to stop looking into it, and killed him before he actually hired me."

Rico's rental purred south along Highway One, hills on the left and ocean on the right, with the dark man following him at a distance.

"But I did get hired. Boris Luftin wants me to solve the murder and figure out what's going on with the rabid robotics. Ol' Elon Baby has a great idea. He's gonna start making his own chips and get away from problems with outside vendors. Maybe I *do* need one of his sexy trucks."

The road got narrower and more twisty, and closer to the edge of the cliff that dropped hundreds of feet to the ocean. Rico and his tail drove sedately to the south along the ocean-edge road.

Rico's conversation with himself continued. "So now I have good and bad chips, and as soon as I can get them to Yeats we can find out who made what, and maybe get to the bottom of all this crap. And I'm not surprised some bozo wants to keep tabs on me down this road. If I were to suddenly drive off the cliff, they'd win. There would be no investigation into who made what chips, and the bad guys win, at least up to some indeterminate future time."

As Rico drove down Highway One he kept his eye on the rear-view mirror, which the trailing car's driver interpreted as Rico watching the scenery. Rico said to himself, "I'll bet a shiny nickel this guy tries to run me off the road, somewhere along here where there's a good drop to the ocean with no guard rail."

Heading into the Big Sur area, Rico noticed there were no guard rails along much of the road. Even at drastic drop-offs there was nothing to prevent him from turning right and zipping several hundred feet straight down onto the rocks at the edge of the ocean.

"This is what that bozo behind me is looking for," said Rico to himself. "Shit! Here he comes!"

In the car following Rico the dark man sped up, zipped into the left lane to speed past Rico's rental car exactly where there was a huge drop-off and no guard rail on the right side of the highway, and then the dark man made a sudden swerve to the right. Rico saw him coming and as soon as the following car was in the left lane Rico stood on the brakes. The dark man made his swerve, hit nothing, and then desperately tried to swerve back to the left. His car's rear tires had skidded to the left from his sudden swerve to the right, and this positioned the dark man's car facing nearly directly off the cliff. Unfortunately for him, the car's rear wheels were still trying to drive the car at sixty miles an hour, and with the front of the dark man's car now aimed over the cliff, that's where it went.

No one else was on the road to see this except for Rico Morgan. He stopped his car, which didn't take long because he was already nearly stopped from his hard braking. He got out of the car and peered over the edge of the cliff. He was in time to see the car as it hit and split to pieces on the huge rocks at the foot of the cliff. Clearly there was nothing Rico could do for the man, nor could he find out who he had been, so he went back to his rental car and continued his drive south. He said to himself, "That poor bastard really didn't think that through, did he."

As he had told Yeats, Rico was not carrying a cell phone, so at the first small town he came to he notified the local police he saw a car drive off the cliff not far north. He didn't tell them the car tried to run him off the road. "This guy came roaring past me and zip, flew off the side of the road. I couldn't get down to help him, but with a drop like that I'm pretty sure I would not have been able to help the guy."

"You're sure it was a man driving?"

"Yes, I got a good look at him as he went by. Then he swerved to the right and off the cliff he went."

The cops took it in stride. They'd seen and heard it before many times. Plenty of drunks fouled up the scenery every year by doing what this joker had done. The cops knew there was nothing they could do, so they took Rico's contact information and sent him on his way.

Before Rico left the little village he found a post office, went inside, packed the four chips into a USPS Priority Mail box and sent them to I. Yeats Prunzalot in Boise, Idaho. He included a note that read, "Find out who made these ASAP. Also find out who went off Highway One today just north of this post-office address."

Rico continued his drive to the south, stopped for the night at a motel in Ventura, had a leisurely dinner at the motel's cafeteria, got up the next morning and made his airline connection in Los Angeles. He flew to Missoula, Montana, picked up his old Dodge factory hot rod from the long-term parking and drove south to his home just north of Salmon, Idaho.

There were numerous telephone messages waiting for him at home. Rico lived in a region that had no cell-phone service, one more reason for him to shun the 'picture phones,' as his doctor friend called them. His land line was connected to a normal phone-message machine. The most recent message was from Yeats. Rico called him. "Yeats, what did you find out about those four chips?"

"Ah, Mr. Morgan, I have found out the so-called good chips were made by Fortune Technologies. That's the company in Casablanca. The so-called bad chips were also made by Fortune Technologies. The only difference is there is some code written into the bad chips that indeed counts the number of cycles of its operation. I have not yet been able to determine what the programming following that cycle count does, but it is entirely different from that preceding it."

"Yeats, that's excellent. I'm amazed you found out so much in such a short time."

"Oh yes indeedy, thank you Mr. Morgan. As you probably know I was preparing for it, kind sir, so it was not all that difficult." Yeats' thick Indian accent came to the fore as he took Rico's compliment.

"Did you find out who was in that car that zinged off the road?"

"Yes, kind sir. I wondered if there had been any funny business along that road, but there was no indication of it in the police report."

"I didn't tell the cops everything. The gentleman tried to run me off the road, bungled it, and went over himself. So, who was he?"

"His name was Tripp Anfall," replied Yeats. "He was a sort of private investigator of questionable repute who had a business address in the Sacramento area. He was fifty-two years old, and had several counts against him from the law-enforcement people over the past few years."

"So, a hired thug."

"That would seem to be correct, kind sir."

"So when do I leave for Casablanca?"

" I have your tickets purchased for a departure in three days."

"Crikey, Yeats, I was joking! Don't I get any time home?"

"Kind sir, I gave you two days."

CHAPTER 12
Big City

Rico Morgan walked the streets of Casablanca the evening he arrived there. He wore his trademark black jeans, plaid shirt and Harris-Tweed sports jacket. Under the jacket was his Charles Daly Hi-Power copy in 9mm in a modern Bachman Slide Number 101 holster from Old West Reproductions. He doubted he'd need the pistol, but brought it at the suggestion of I. Yeats Prunzalot, seconded by G. William Kers, both members of Rico's Boise Control advisory panel, both of whom had spent time in the Casablanca area in northwest Africa. He also doubted it was legal to be packin' iron, but wasn't about to ask anyone. Bad people anywhere in the world can get and carry handguns, Rico knew, and he wasn't about to let local laws stop him from keeping himself alive. Not when he was after a potential murderer.

"I'm hungry," he said to himself. He was walking along Ait Afalman street. "But I don't want to eat a foul man...." "But heck, I don't know a soul here nor do I know where I can get anything, much less a foul man, to eat. Someone at the airport said this street was the place to go to get food, but it's nearly deserted but for a few stalls selling what might be considered to be raw food. Ah! Maybe there...." Down the next street Rico saw a sign that looked like it might be for a restaurant. On closer inspection it turned out to be a public laundry.

When Rico landed in Casablanca at Mohammed V airport he rented a car, then drove about a dozen miles to his hotel and checked in. That evening he chose to walk around rather than drive, to get a feeling for the city and its inhabitants. "This'll be lots more fun than driving to...I don't know where." And so he walked around at some length, exploring.

Rico was surprised at the size of Casablanca. He thought it was a tiny town, but found out its immediate population was in excess of three million. The local area around the city contained nearly seven million souls. "I thought this was a hick town. Heck, it's a huge city! And look at all the industry here! Aerospace, even. What a surprise."

Rico consulted his map. "Why do so many names down here sound like someone hawking up phlegm? Look at this map," Rico said to himself. He was carrying a folding paper map of the Casablanca area, and also had a similar map on his cell phone, which Yeats insisted he carry. "Was this place built by ancient men with congested lungs and crud in their throats? Or is it just me, not being used to Arabic names? Hay Hassani. (Yeah? I'm Hassani...whadda ya want?) Maarif. (Patooie!) Lissasfa. (Patooie again!) Ain Chock. (Or is it Up Chuck?) Sidi Othmani. (I'm already siddin' on the ottoman.) Here's a good one...Tit Mellil. (Mellow tits?) I think I'm out of my element here in Casablanca. Hope there's a good bar or two around, after I get some dinner."

Rico's mind continued having fun on the map. "Let's see...Avenue des Far. Well, I've got dis far. Might as well go farther." He walked a few more streets and finally saw the ultimate bar/restaurant he'd never go in. "What's this...*Le*

Poisson? No way am I gonna eat at a place called 'the poison'! Somethin' fishy about that name. Surely there must be something better!"

Walking along the Boulevard Ben Abdellah Rico found a splendid French restaurant called La Bavaroise, in which he had an excellent dinner of French cuisine, wine and all. It was not cheap, but the food was excellent. Talking to himself again, he said, "This Casablanca place is mostly Arabs with a bunch of remaining French influence here and there. The French cookin' here ain't half bad. Gotta remember this place. Maybe bring Sally...er, can't do that any more, can I. Okay, maybe bring Roxy here. If I ever see her again. Okay, I'll bring Mole here. Where *IS* that bastard?" Rico desperately wanted to have his friend Modesto Pincata Buena with him on this journey, but it was not to be. Foregoing a postprandial visit to any of the local bars, Rico made his way back to his hotel, the Odyssee Center, which was a short walk northwest from the French restaurant.

Later that night he drove his rental car south, back past the airport. He found the Fortune Technologies factory right where his people at Boise Control had pinpointed it for him. Fortune Technologies was roughly fifteen miles south of Rico's hotel, on the south side of the big airport. This made sense, Rico noted, because Farchex' customers were mostly not in Casablanca and the robotics and chips had to be shipped out of the country, and what could be more convenient than having the factory near the airport. The airport served the world.

He drove past the factory and noted there was still lots of activity inside at going on ten o'clock in the evening. Rico wanted to get a closer look, so he parked his car a block away and walked back. Some of the windows were open to the night air and were not far from what passed for a sidewalk. He carefully peered in at several of the open windows and got a surprise. Clearly good work was going on late at night, which was not surprising for a viable company with world-wide connections, but the surprise was in the work force. To a man – and some women – the workers were all Chinese. All the talk that Rico overheard was in the sing-song Mandarin tongue that he'd heard several times in other parts of the world, and clearly recognized. There was no English or French or Arabic spoken at all. A large fence kept him from going completely around the building, but everywhere he looked he saw and heard the same foreign tongue being spoken.

Rico walked back to his rental and drove back to his hotel.

Early the next morning as he had coffee and rolls in his room he pondered the situation, talking to himself as usual. "I know this guy Farchex is making both good and bogus chips as well as solid, functional robotics machinery. As I saw last night it's not a tiny nor a lazy company. I wondered why he settled here in Casablanca, and the answer seems to be that he can get Chinese for cheap labor here and do that easier than in any EU country, and far easier than in the U.S.

"Now, then...if I confront him with the fact that he's making both good and bad chips he'll deny it, and claim the defaced ones were not done within his company. Ideally I'd like to sneak into the factory and find some chips fresh off the assembly line that have been buggered. That won't be easy. Stands to reason all the chips he uses in his robotics assemblies are nothing but good, unbuggered chips. So the bad ones will not be on the assembly line for the robotics. The bad chips must be pulled from wherever they're made and then routed to a lab or a different room where the code gets corrupted and the name defaced. A small room or facility near the output of the chip manufacturing area is where this'll be going on. There, or outside the factory completely. I need to find that." Rico considered the possibilities. "Once I verify the chips with the bad code come from Farchex I have a case against the bastard and can take action against him."

Rico was plotting his next move when his cell phone rang. It was Yeats in Boise, Idaho, some 5,500 miles away.

"It's midnight here in Boise, kind sir. I presume it's eight o'clock in the morning there?"

"That's correct, Yeats. What do you have?"

"I am sorry to tell you the Farchex chip manufactory is in Portugal, not with the robotics factory in Casablanca. The good news is it's in the same time zone, only about two hundred and fifty miles north. That is less than one hour's flying time."

"That's okay, Yeats. That solves one of the mysteries here, actually. I wondered how he, Farchex, could bugger the chips if they were made here in Casablanca. So after I'm done with this rogue here I'll go up there and try to get some information on the chips, how they're made, and so on. I'll let you know when I'm done here in north Africa and you can arrange for me to fly up there, okay? What city, by the way?"

"The city is Faro, right on the south coast of Portugal. It has a significant airport. Mixed in with the rampant tourist visitation sites there is a small house in which the chips are made and they are then flown to Casablanca. Yes indeedy, kind sir, when you need to go to Faro just let me know and I'll arrange a flight. Now, then, there is some additional information about Mr. Farchex circulating on the, er, hidden channels." Yeats was a brilliant hacker and could easily get into confidential sources, which he commonly called hidden channels. They were hidden from most people but not from Yeats. "The information tends to confirm that a bribe was sent by Mr. Farchex to a gentleman in high office in Australia. The bribe to this high official was for him to make sure a particular new factory got destroyed by the increasingly bad wildfires in the north of Australia."

"Do you know what the factory made, or any details about it?"

"It was largely Chinese owned and was going to refine tellurium, used in making computer chips and solar panels."

"Hmmm. Why in blazes did Farchex want that destroyed? Whose hidden channels, if I can be so bold?"

"Those of the Clearinghouse Information Agency," replied Yeats.

"Got it," replied Rico. "I wonder if a certain, er 'Clearinghouse' agent friend of mine, who is supposedly in Australia, knows anything about that?"

"I have no idea, Mr. Morgan. Good night...or good morning, as it is there."

"Thanks, Yeats. Go to bed, and good night to you as well."

Rico pondered the problem still more. "First, I've gotta get to Mr. Farchex. Somehow wangle an opportunity to interview Farchex to try to find out why he's making both good and bad chips. He'll deny it of course. Might not even see me, but I have a way to at least get in his face. Once I do that, how can I get more out of him? Maybe I can let him know the CIA has info on his bribing some government cat in Australia."

CHAPTER 13
Casablanca

Roxy Roades and Mary Teslin arrived in Casablanca early in the day, checked into their hotel and took a nap. The endless-seeming flight was finally over, and they were exhausted by the change in time, the long day flying west chasing the sun, and the shock of changed cultures, from Australia to Morocco.

When they woke, the evening was upon them. "Mary," said Roxy, "what say we go out on the town and get us some booze and some dinner."

"Excellent idea," said Mary through several yawns. "But where to go?"

"I know of a place, not too far from here, that'll give you the shivers. I always wanted to go there if I was ever in this town. Let's go to Rick's Café!"

"Okay, but...what is it anyway?"

"You ever see the old movie *Casablanca*? The cafe that Humphrey Bogart ran was called Rick's Café Américain and some folks have duplicated it here, right up the street from this hotel. I'd heard about it but never dreamed I'd be in Casablanca to go there."

"I've never seen that movie, so I don't know much about it."

"Mary, how could you!? I've seen it a dozen times. It's a love story within a tale of the Nazi occupation of French Morocco, and all that within the aura of a bar in Casablanca where everything happens. It stars Bogey with Ingrid Bergman as the leading lady. The famous quotation 'Play it, Sam' comes from that movie. It's usually bungled as 'Play it again, Sam,' but 'again' is never said by anyone in the movie."

"Okay. Sounds good to me. Let's go visit Humphrey Bogart."

"He's dead, you know...."

"Oh. Well, maybe someone else famous will be there."

The two women went out, got a cab, and were taken to Rick's Café. They had a modest bit of food in one of the rear areas removed from the main bar, had some great drinks, and were admiring the intimate and classic decor of the place. A piano was near them. Roxy wondered if 'Sam' was going to come in and play "As Time Goes By."

Suddenly Roxy said, "Oh! My! God! It can't be!"

A man had just walked in and sat down at the bar.

"What?" Mary asked. "Did you just see Bogey's ghost?"

"Even better. How'm I gonna do this...? Got it! Mary, there's someone I know very well over there at the bar. I'm going to go up and say hello, and I'll do it like one of the ghosts of this great old bar. Stay here!"

Earlier that evening Rico Morgan walked from his hotel west to the end of the block, crossed Avenue des Far onto Rue el Oraibi Jilali, headed north to the big boulevard, and followed that toward the sea until he got to Boulevard des Almohades. Rico walked to the northwest along Almohades past the waterfront area, and past all the near-shore activity of the bustling port of Casablanca. When he got just past the Rue Mourabitine, which led onto the dock area to the northeast,

Rico turned left onto the Boulevard Sour Jdid, and a few steps took him to the destination he promised himself he'd be sure to visit if he ever got to Casablanca, Rick's Café. This restaurant was inspired by one of Rico's favorite old movies, *Casablanca*.

When Rico walked in the door he half expected to see Humphrey Bogart's ghost, Sam at the piano, and several prominent Nazis in the room. He wouldn't have been surprised if the entire inside of the place had turned black-and-white, no colors whatsoever, just as in the old movie. It didn't, nor did he see Nazis or ghosts.

"This is amazing," he replied. "It's not all black and white in here, I actually see colors, but it sure looks like the 'gin joint' from that famous movie. What was it called? Oh, yes. *Casablanca*!"

Rico went to the bar and ordered an appropriate drink, gin on the rocks. He sat drinking and musing, soaking up the ambiance of the place, thinking of the atmosphere of that 1942 movie, experiencing it here in living color. No one was at the piano, but it was there. He glanced over at the roulette wheel. It was there, too. His mind took him through some of the famous scenes and quotations from the movie, images and words still alive eight decades later.

Rico Morgan sat dreaming, staring across the bar, nursing his gin, regretting he didn't have a white dinner jacket on. Suddenly a woman's voice spoke to him.

"Of all the gin joints in all the towns in all the world, he walks into mine."

Rico, stunned nearly out of his mind, his gin glass in his hand, slowly turned around and looked into the beautiful face of Roxy Roades. He stared. The world stopped for a second. Everything turned to black and white, and he was suddenly wearing a white dinner jacket.

He turned, slowly, set his gin glass on the bar, stood up, turned back to Roxy, looked deep into her eyes and said, "Here's looking at you, kid."

In a second they were in each other's arms. The kiss went on forever.

Slowly the room turned from black and white to full Technicolor as he and Roxy finally broke their nearly endless kiss.

Rico remarked, "I have nothing to say other than 'What the heck are you doing here?', which I'll bet..."

"...a shiny nickel," broke in Roxy.

"...Yes, that, I'll bet a shiny nickel you have exactly the same question for me."

"You win the nickel, Rico."

"I can't believe this. Here we both are in this amazing city, both so far from home. What are the chances you'd be here? Or I'd be here? And at the same time?" Rico picked up his gin and took a slug.

Roxy, still smiling from her rousing reception, said, "Mighty slim chances, pilgrim! But I won't be all that surprised if we're both onto the same mystery. That's half logical. So, why are you here?" She took the gin out of Rico's hand and took a sip.

"Well, I'm chasing down a bad computer chip, tryin' to find out who made it, what they did to it, and who might have killed someone because of it. How about you?"

"I'm here with Mary Teslin, sittin' over there behind the wall and hiding from us. We're trying to find out why some clown in Casablanca paid off a government official in Australia to burn down a metalloid refinery. Why don't you come and join us...if you're alone...?"

"Sure, I'll...WHAT?! Burned down a factory in Australia?! August Farchex!"

"WHAT?!" Roxy was as nonplussed as Rico. "We're after the same guy?! What the hell!"

"Yeah, the guy has a factory here and it supplies the chips to this company that hired me out of Atlanta. And I just found out he bribed someone to make sure that factory was destroyed."

"Now how in hell do you know that? We learned it only two days ago."

"Er, ah, that is, um...I have my sources. So you were the one who found that out?"

"Actually Mary found it. She's new but mighty sharp. Let's go meet her...if you're alone. You never said. No Sally? No Mole?"

"Yes, I'm alone. I'm totally alone. Sally left me because, well, because of misunderstandings and some differences of opinion. All my fault for asking her something I should not have asked. Mole's in France, or Spain, or for all I know Timbuktu, with his new lady friend."

"Oh, no! Sally left you? Rico, was it because of us? Because...I never told her!"

"Not exactly about us. Well, maybe a little bit. She guessed right about us. As she put it, it was something about our sore crotches and our glow-in-the-dark blushes when we were all together at my place. But mostly because I demanded to know how she arranged that airplane ride and the limo that brought us from Caracas all the way to my front door. She had something hidden from me and, well, it wasn't a nice argument. You must be Mary." Rico and Roxy arrived at the table where Mary Teslin was sitting. She was still slightly red in the face about the way Roxy greeted Rico.

Roxy did the intros. "Mary, this is Rico Morgan. You may remember his name came up when we were talking with the guitarist at that bar."

"Hi, Rico. I'm Mary Teslin. I work with Roxy."

"Mary," said Roxy, "Rico knows what we do. He and I worked together a time or two, most recently in Caracas."

"Oh!" Mary was surprised. "On that thing with the gold and the big stone and the crooked leaders in Caracas? Wow! That's impressive. I read about that somewhere."

"Probably in the brief I filed," said Roxy.

"Okay," said Rico. "We're here after the same guy, August Farchex. You two are here to verify he sent the bribe to Australia."

At that, Mary looked at Roxy with confusion on her face. "Did you tell him?"

"No. He has sneaks that tell him things."

Rico continued. "I want to find out why some of his computer chips are bogus, and see what he says about it. His company is huge. I was there last night. All his workers are Chinese, so there's a language barrier there for us."

"Not for me," said Mary.

Rico and Roxy stared at her. "Eh?" said Rico, dumfounded.

"Yes, I speak Mandarin. My mother was Chinese, and then I studied it in college."

"Well, that'll be helpful." Rico was still amazed. "To me the Chinese language is like an alien came here and started to talk to me but I couldn't understand a word, and then he took me off to Mars because I couldn't say no."

"Have some more gin, Rico," replied Roxy.

"Yes, that too," he said. "Anyway, is there some way we can help each other?"

"I could do an interview," said Roxy. I have the papers, which is how I interviewed the head spook in Australia."

"What did that do for you in Australia?" Rico asked.

"Really not much," said Roxy.

Mary added, "We learned more by busting into his house."

"That's where Mary found the letter to Drapcox from Farchex. We photo'ed it and sent the info and pix back to Washington...oh. So that's how Yeats saw it."

"I never said that," said Rico.

"But he did. So that's how you know."

"Something like that."

"What the hell are you two talking about?" asked Mary.

"Rico has a little spook, who looks into our stuff. That's the way that Rico learns. He's always up to snuff." Roxy beamed at her instant rhyme.

Rico chuckled and said, "Have some more wine, Rox."

"Why don't you two get a room. I'll sit here with my daiquiri."

Roxy said, "Er, mummum dedahh kawonker stooch."

Rico said, "Jahaba daba doodie kaflunchingrabber."

Mary looked up at each of them and said, "Oops!"

Roxy recovered enough to say, "So let's have a drink, everyone. Time to celebrate! We can discuss our jobs tomorrow."

Some time later when the trio was somewhat better oiled, Roxy noted, "I was surprised at the size of Casablanca. After seeing that old movie I thought this would be just a small town."

"So was I. It actually has more people in the urban area than Chicago, more's the surprise," said Rico. "By the way, the movie Casablanca was filmed entirely in Hollywood."

"Really!" exclaimed Roxy.

Mary joined in. "Roxy said it was filmed in 1942. The war was still on, and there were probably real Nazis here, so they couldn't have made the movie here."

"Yes," said Rico. "Real Nazis and the French occupation forces. The U.S. had just entered the war...but still, there was no need nor any sense in trying to film it on location. Hollywood at the time was the center of all things cinema, at least in the U.S. So everyone thinks Casablanca was a tiny town based on that movie. But nobody's been here to see this place, and if they have, no one's said how huge this city is. Guys, I'm gonna make my way back to my hotel. I'm at the Odyssee Center. Where are you staying?"

"We're at the Oum Palace Hotel."

"And Spa," said Mary. "Don't forget the spa."

"You're a short walk from me. So I'll call you, cell phone to cell phone – Yeats made me bring one – in the morning. We can foregather and discuss strategies in a more sober venue."

"Burp!" said Roxy.

"Duhhh!" said Rico.

"I still think you guys should get a room." Mary didn't blush. Roxy and Rico did.

CHAPTER 14
Background

The next day Rico met with Roxy and Mary over a late breakfast. At Rico's suggestion they'd walked about half a mile to the east from their hotels, which were essentially next to each other, to a restaurant called BlueBerry Casablanca. Rico said, "It's a relatively new and unheralded beanery, but I have high hopes for it." As luck had it, the food was excellent and the prices reasonable. After they'd eaten a resounding breakfast, the serious discussion began. Rico kicked it off.

"*Amigas,* here's what I know. This fellow Farchex had a plant destroyed in Australia that was refining tellurium, which is used for making computer chips. I don't know another thing about that factory, but it doesn't stand to reason Farchex would destroy a source of something he needs to make his chips."

"We can help you there," replied Roxy. "The factory was run by, and largely financed by, the Chinese. They were going to be able to sell tellurium at a cheaper price to U.S. buyers than the same product directly out of China. Note I said U.S. buyers, and that because of the upcoming U.S. tariffs on stuff imported from China. China's the main source of tellurium in the world today."

"Aha! So destroying that source of tellurium outside China automatically imposes a higher price on the product to U.S. buyers, because they have to continue buying direct from China and pay the tariff. But anyone outside the U.S., like Farchex, can still buy tellurium cheaply from China. No tariff! By destroying the Aussie plant he destroyed a cheap source of tellurium and by extension cheap computer chips for his U.S. rivals, namely Luftin-Borlew Industries in Atlanta."

"But didn't you tell me that company does not make its own chips?" Roxy asked.

"Yes, but Elon Musk at Tesla is about to start making his own chips, and logic sez those home-grown chips would be bought by Luftin-Borlew, and also by anyone else who wants to have U.S.-made chips with the total control that gives them. With the high price of importing tellurium, currently the best viable source being in China, it's far cheaper to buy chips from Farchex here in Casablanca. Something I haven't told you is there's good evidence of collusion between the founder of Luftin-Borlew, Boris Luftin, and August Farchex."

Mary got it first. With a flip of her red hair she asked, "Why would Boris Luftin want to drive up prices of supplies to his own company? If he's in cahoots with this badger here in Casablanca, it makes no sense he wants to impose higher prices on his company's product."

"Ah, but it does, especially if he wants to destroy his own company!"

Roxy asked, "Why in hell would he want to do that?"

"I think I know," said Rico, "but I need to test something with fatso Farchex first. I want to establish what I suspect, that he and Luftin are in fact working together to do just that."

"Why not just sell the company, or close it down? Would that not be cheaper?" Mary asked.

"Not any more," replied Rico. "We found a major problem with Luftin-Borlew from a few years ago. The company was about to go bust, but a huge loan came to save them from Portugal. The chip-making part of Farchex' operation is in Portugal, and my people verified Farchex was the source of that loan of several years ago.

"So Farchex," Rico continued, "essentially owns a good chunk of Luftin-Borlew Industries in Atlanta. But almost no one knows it. So if Luftin-Borlew, also known as L-B, owes Farchex a huge debt, which is now hidden but which would surface if any attempt were made to sell the company, the sale price of L-B goes to pot. But if the L-B company is destroyed because of its poor products, there are insurance policies and bank deals that will save the share-holders a ton of money. Boris Luftin, the only survivor of the two founders, is a major shareholder, as you might expect. He doesn't want to have to pay Farchex what Luftin's company still owes Farchex. I don't begin to understand the workings, but my people at Boise Control told me the best deal is for the company to be ruined, not sold."

Mary replied, "The ruined company would eventually be sold, but of course the price would be extremely low, like in the basement. The old company name would be worthless on the market. The machinery and tooling could be reused, and the company renamed, but they'd be starting from the ground up to try to make a name for themselves. So the big winner would be the company's main competitor right now, which I'd bet is Fortune Technologies."

"Bingo!" replied Rico. "If Farchex and Luftin are not in collusion to have this Casablanca company overshadow the Atlanta company, none of this makes sense. By keeping the U.S. price of tellurium high the best computer-chip buys come not from within the U.S., but from Portugal. That's why Farchex paid to have that factory destroyed in Australia, to keep his profits up. The clever Chinese were trying to circumvent the tariff by making a plant in Australia to refine and sell the stuff to the U.S. cheaper than the same product refined in China. And now with the new plant destroyed, that idea's dead."

"There's another aspect here," said Mary. "Farchex has stuck his finger into the eye of the Chinese by destroying a factory that was going to make good money for the Chinese. If they find out, Farchex is screwed. Especially with all his Chinese help here."

"Good point," said Rico.

"Yes, he is," agreed Roxy. Then she asked, "Why do you suspect they're in collusion?"

"Luftin told me a story about a meeting between himself and Farchex when they were back in college. Luftin's wife later told a slightly different version that revealed they knew each other far better than Luftin let on to me. Also, when the L-B company was about to go belly up a couple years ago Farchex provided the funds to keep them going. He'd hardly do that to a hated rival."

"And how do you propose to find out if they're in collusion?"

"Simple." Rico told them his trick.

Mary asked, "Okay if it works, but what will he do once he's aware you're a private eye looking into his collusion with an American CEO, and realizes you've just won a major victory? How can he fight back?"

"He's already killed a man because that man hired me. Or if it wasn't Farchex who hired the hit on the CEO and the attempt on me...."

"What?!" Roxy spilled some of her coffee.

"Someone tried to run me off the road. Didn't work. If it wasn't Farchex who hired the hit, then it had to have been orchestrated by Boris Luftin back in Atlanta. If Luftin hired the hit then this guy Farchex will probably do nothing when we confront him with his collusion with Farchex. He has nothing to lose because of it at this point. All he did was befriend the owner of a rival company, nothing illegal there. If Farchex did hire the hit, or had a hand in it, he might run."

"How about the bribe to the intelligence guy in Australia?" Mary asked.

"Hmmm. I think Farchex would run if faced with that info," said Rico. "Especially if it's mentioned, truthful or not, that the Chinese are about to be informed of that little fact. They'd probably come after him for it."

Roxy said, "I'd guess that fight's going to be fought between Australia and this guy, with maybe – probably – input from China, and of course the other investors like Elon."

Mary said, "This guy's toast because of the letter we found. We really should have taken it. It could be said our photos are fake. But then, we could also have forged the letter if we had it."

"That's right," replied Roxy. "What we need is witnesses hearing this guy admit to the bribe, or a seizing of his banking assets which would prove he sent the money to the Aussie guy."

"How about one of you posing as a Moroccan bank auditor? Get a look at the files." Rico waved to the waitress for more coffee.

"Yuk," said Roxy. "I doubt that would float."

Mary suggested, "It might be a good idea to contact the local police about him before we go see him. Whadda ya think?"

"I think it's a waste of time," said Roxy. "We have no real proof to get 'em involved. How about we all go and throw everything we have at him, see what he does?"

"What is it we're really trying to do?" asked Rico. "Let's say he's guilty of everything, the bribe, the bad chips, even the murder. What do we have on him and what can we do with it? If we throw it in his face he can deny it all, and we have only the letter you guys saw to verify the bribe. As to the chips, I know the bogus chips were made by his company but have no way of determining if the chip diddling was done by him, or by some outside outfit."

"Here's a thought," said Roxy. "What if we go to Portugal and have a serious look at the arrangements there. Didn't you tell me, Rico, that your man determined the chips are made in a small house there? That's less daunting than to try to attack this guy in this huge factory here in Casablanca."

"Yes it is," said Rico. "We might even be able to break in, and find the evidence we need. I could look for bad chips being reprogrammed at the source, and you could look for banking evidence of the bribe. Assuming the accounting books show it...."

"Er, could someone hack into his bank statements and verify the sending of the bribe?" Roxy smiled at Rico and sipped her coffee.

"Guys, I had too much booze last night – again. Cain't think of nuttin' for myself. I'll get Yeats on that immediately."

Roxy added, "And if he can't find anything, what do we have?"

Rico answered, "Hopefully a set of good and bad chips, which we can come back here and stuff in August Farchex's face." Rico was warming to the idea of a trip to Portugal.

"There's no rush to confront this guy, not at this point in time. Are your people doing anything about the guy in Australia?"

"We have no idea," said Mary. "We're essentially mushrooms."

"Can your man Yeats find out anything about that, about our people in Washington having confronted that head-spook guy in Australia with receipt of a bribe?" Roxy asked.

"Dunno. We'll see." Rico pulled out his cell phone, punched the number for Yeats in Idaho, and immediately cancelled it. "It's three in the morning there now. I can get to him this afternoon. Meantime, let's consider a fast trip to Portugal, and let's talk about it outside."

The trio left BlueBerry Casablanca restaurant and went for a walk. They headed southeast down Rue de Lille until they got to Rue de Provins, headed east past the bank at the bend until they got to the wooded park there just across the Boulevard Emile Zola. The park entrance was hidden, and no one seemed to know how to get into it. Finally they found a way in and walked under the trees discussing their options. An hour later they headed home, taking in the sights of the bustling big city.

Back at the hotel that afternoon Rico communicated with Yeats in Boise and asked him to look into CIA's challenging the head of ASIO in Australia with receipt of a bribe. As usual, Yeats had already done that and had the information for Rico.

About the trip to Faro, Yeats told Rico that commercial flights from Casablanca to Faro were available, but took seven hours to fly 250 miles.

"Bullshit!" said Rico. "We'll have to see if we can get an air taxi out of the local small airport."

The answer was that no, they could not, because of customs regulations. That left Rico with one option, though not a cheap one. He phoned the women at their hotel.

"Well, kids, we're gonna charter a jet to take us to Faro and back. The good news is the flight takes about an hour. The bad news is we can't get a local air taxi, I can't rent an airplane I can fly, and the charter's gonna cost about five grand."

"We can cover that," said Roxy. "I guess the problem is that it's two different countries, with customs and so on between 'em."

"Yes, and the commercial flights can't make a dime if they go up outa here and then come right back down into Faro. So they have to take a round-about route from here to some place like Berlin or London and then back down to Faro. We could drive, but that sucks. It's many hours and many miles. So it's hire a charter. Can we leave tomorrow? I'll have the charter take us, and come back the next day to get us. How's that sound? Does that give us enough time?"

"I think we might need two days, or rather two nights to do our work."

"Roger that. I'll set it up."

"Good. What'd Yeats say?"

"He found out a payment of thirty thousand euros just went from Farchex's account in Faro to the account of one Miles Drapcox, the intelligence guy in Australia. About two months ago a payment of ten thousand euros went to the same guy. So we've got that to shove in Farchex's face. Yes, the account was traceable from the Portugal bank back to Farchex's account here in Casablanca."

"So, we've got him on that, anyway. Now for the chips!"

CHAPTER 15
Faro

The Cessna Citation M2 took off at ten out of Mohammed V airport the next morning carrying Rico, Mary and Roxy from Casablanca northward over the two-hundred-fifty miles across the Atlantic ocean from Africa to Europe. About an hour later it set them down in Faro, Portugal. The town is part of a group of small towns all along the southern coast of Portugal in what's called the Algarve region, which basically is all of southern Portugal. Faro is a tourist town but also has some industry, and about 65,000 people. The coast has some fantastic views, rocks, cliffs, and decent beaches. The trio got a good look at some of it as the Cessna jet settled in to the long runway at Faro.

It was a simple matter to rent a car and, following the directions and GPS guidance Rico got from I. Yeats Prunzalot of Boise Control, the trio drove easily to the address of Farchex's chip manufactory in Faro.

Much if not most of Faro was ancient, with extremely narrow streets never designed for cars, many of them now one-way, many others prohibiting all motor traffic. The factory was on a narrow street on the northeast side of the town, in a typical square-block building of two stories with a flat roof. It might have been a residence long ago, but was now a factory. There were other stores and other places nearby that might have been manufacturing facilities or perhaps residences in the neighborhood. A furniture store was just down the street. Another outlet sold refrigerators.

The doorway of the chip maker had a simple small plaque showing the name of Fortune Technologies. The trio passed through the entry door into a twenty-foot square reception area lined with shelves, some boxes, a cupboard or two, and a large steel cabinet near one corner of the room. At a desk in the middle of the room sat a middle-aged secretary typing something on a computer keyboard. She greeted them in Portuguese. Roxy answered in Spanish and asked if she spoke English.

"Yes I do," replied the woman. She was in her middle forties, trim and neat, wearing a simple white blouse and slacks. Her graying hair was kept in a tight bun at the back of her head. "What can I do for you?"

"We understand you make computer chips here," Roxy stated.

"Yes we do. What is it you're actually looking for?"

Rico took over the story. "We have a small robotics factory in the U.S. and would like to secure a series of dedicated chips for our machines. We need a programmable master chip, or chip set as it may be, that we can alter to do what we need it to do."

"Sir, and madams, we can most likely provide you with what you need. Can you provide us with some idea of your specific needs?"

"Common programming, able to handle simple instructions, one that can be reprogrammed to some extent. As I said, we want it to run some robotics for us. We'll need about a thousand, but we'd really like to buy a few samples to see if they are exactly what we are looking for."

"No problem. We have some that are being made for another robotics company and I think these will serve you quite well." She hauled up a sample chip from the depths of her desk and Rico immediately recognized it as being exactly like one of the supposedly good ones that he got at the Tesla factory.

"Can you provide us with several, say three, of those? We need to run some parallel tests and odd types of programming."

"Yes, certainly. One moment, please." She went to a cupboard behind her desk and pulled out two more of the chips. "Will there be anything else at the moment?"

Rico decided to chance it. "My friend here has a nephew who has a quirky toy. It's a small robot with voice, facial expressions, simple stuff like that. Nothing complex. I mean it doesn't jump and dance. But it's kind of strange. It does its thing for most of the time in a specific character, but then after a few days or weeks switches to a totally different character. Do you folks know how that chip is made? Do you have anything like it?"

The woman receptionist glanced quickly at a steel cabinet in the far corner of the room and then back to Rico. "Sir," she said, "I really have no idea what you're talking about. We have in the past made a similar device for computer games, but we no longer make such a thing. Now if you have everything you need...."

Rico paid, took the three chips, and the three friends left the establishment. When they were in the car heading for the hotel they'd booked, Rico said it first. "We have to hit that steel cabinet."

Mary and Roxy said in unison, "Yep."

That afternoon Mary suggested a trip to the beach. "We might go here," she said, pointing on the computer's satellite image at a section of the beach that was south of the airport and could be reached by car. "We might be able to drive down to the east and get away from people."

Rico looked at the satellite image. "Looks like a lot of folks go there. I suspect it's a tourist trap. I see what look like houses all the way down to the southeast end."

"Yuk," said Mary. "You're right." She looked again at the on-screen image. "I see that. That's no fun. Not even in a tourist town like this. I ain't no friggin' tourist!"

"From what I've read," continued Rico, if you want a beach without people take the ferry to the 'deserted island,' called Ilha Deserta, actually Praia da Baretta, because not many folks go there."

"Where do you want to go, Rico?" asked Roxy.

"I'm far more interested in this hilly, forested piece of land about ten or fifteen miles north of here. Looks like I can drive the N2 highway up into it, and then park somewhere and walk around to see what it's like. It's the sort of thing not many tourists would do, which suits me fine. I might find a biker up there with a trials machine, but I can avoid the bike trails and get into some interesting country."

Roxy said, "Well, we have only one rental car. So how are we gonna do this?"

"Do you want to go to the beach with Mary?"

"Not really. I could stay here, take a nap. Or go with you to the deep, dark woods."

"Hmmm," said Rico. "Come wiz me to ze casbah!"

"That too."

"How about you guys drop me off at the ferry terminal, and then I can walk home through town when I get back. According to this city map it looks like the ferry terminal is only about a mile from here, on the southwest side of Faro. It'd be nice to walk through this old berg. See what it has to offer the bored non-tourist. It's about a five-mile ferry ride to the deserted island, which I see has a tourist-trap restaurant on it, but heck, I don't have to eat there. So yes, let's do that!"

"Done," said Rico. "*¡Ya nos vamos!*"

"What?" asked Mary.

"Don't mind Rico," said Roxy. "He's just missing his adventure buddy, the Mexican fellow who is...God knows where...right now. Rico said the Spanish version of 'Let's go already!' "

"Isn't that what that Chapstick guy says," asked Mary.

"Chapkis. Greg Chapkis, famous choreographer." Roxy explained. "He's from the Ukraine. It's been suggested he shouts 'Let's go!' at his dance teams to encourage 'em. Might not be true, but it's in the air. So, let's go!"

Rico and Roxy drove Mary to the ferry port where she caught a ride to the deserted island with its five miles of fabulous beach. After they dropped her off Rico and Roxy drove out of town to the north and followed the N2 road for about ten or twelve miles into the surrounding hills. The terrain was steep, covered with trees, and there were many places to turn off and go for a hike. That is what they did.

Mary spent the afternoon at the beach and toward evening caught the ferry back to Faro from the outlying island, once again enjoying the ride through the lovely lagoon with its flocks of wild birds and crystal-clear water. Then she took a leisurely walk through the ancient town. When she arrived back at the hotel the others had not yet returned. They were still in the woods on top of one of the rugged ridges to the north of Faro, deep in the heavily wooded forest.

Roxy and Rico had made a picnic of the outing. They found a good place to park, took a couple of bags with purchased wine, cheese, bread, more wine, and proceeded to hike back away from the road until they were deep inside the woods. There was no one around except for a few wild animals.

Unknown to Rico and Mary, they were being watched.

A squirrel, unseen by the pair, was high in the tree over their heads. He saw the whole performance: watched them come and arrange the blanket under his tree, watched them eat and drink, heard them laugh, saw the touches turn into caresses, saw the first lingering kisses, and overheard their quiet conversation. He saw everything that followed after the woman asked a question.

"Rico, should we be doing this? I mean, you're still officially with Sally, aren't you?"

"I suppose I might be – but if you and I continue as we seem to be continuing here today, we won't be doing anything worse than we've already done. Just compounding a felony."

"I suppose it's like the British say. In for a penny, in for a pounding." Roxy smiled.

"Something like that." Rico kissed her on her blouse where it was tight over her right breast. "Are you going to pound me?"

"Only if you pound me first." She grasped the front of his trousers, rubbed gently, then bent gracefully and kissed him there. She undid his trousers, found what she wanted, and kissed some more.

After a minute or two Roxy sat up and Rico undid her blouse and started his own after-lunch meal. Soon they were both naked. Their passion quickly built and built and finally exploded, leaving them both temporarily satisfied. They lay together side by side, looking up into the branches of the tree. Neither saw the squirrel.

"Pour me some more wine, please." Roxy lay back on the blanket borrowed from the hotel room, naked but for a small towel across her middle. Rico had already put his shorts back on. He poured some of the wine into Roxy's plastic cup.

"Rico, what's going to become of us? I live in Washington, DC, and you live in Idaho. We're two thousand miles apart. How can this ever become really good? I don't think you're about to move to DC and I can't live in Idaho and still be a CIA agent. Are we gonna just get together when we find each other in some odd place on the globe, like two characters in a mystery thriller book? Any ideas?"

"Roxy, I don't know. I'm not going to move to DC. I can't stand the cities and all the people. I love seeing you and being with you, but I can't honestly see how we can have anything resembling a permanent relationship, much though I'd welcome it. Especially right now."

"What do you suppose Sally's doing? Will she come back to you? I know she has a house near your place. Does she own it?"

"Yes, she bought it. I think she might have another place up in Maine or somewhere on the east coast that she rents out. As to what she's doing, I know she went to England. There's a new friend of hers there and I suspect she's with him."

"Zak?"

"Yes."

"So what do we do?"

"How about some more pounding? Or are you hammered out?"

"Not me, Rico. Are you?"

He answered her in the most profound manner possible. The squirrel got tired of watching and jumped to another tree, dropping a pine cone on the lovers as he went.

"What was that?" Roxy asked.

"I don't know and I don't care."

They continued pounding.

Later that night Rico and Roxy left Mary in the hotel room. They wore black outfits. Rico carried his 9mm Hi-Power clone and Roxy had a S&W snubby 38. They'd considered masks and black face paint, but decided against it. The town was dark enough at two ayem local time they thought they could do the job without such tactics. Police presence was essentially nil. They drove to a parking spot a quarter mile and around a corner from the offices of Fortune Technologies in Faro and walked toward it. If they saw anyone coming toward them they'd hold hands and walk close, two lovers going for a stroll late at night. But their task was mischief of a different sort this night.

When they reached the darkened quarters of Fortune Tech it took them less than a minute to open the ancient door lock and enter the front office. There were no lights, no sentries. Roxy scanned the room quickly with her pocket flashlight, keeping it off the windows and damping the beam with her hand. They went to the steel cabinet and found it to be locked. Rico got out his lock pick set again.

"Do you hear that?" asked Roxy. A soft whirring sound began from across the room. She shined her light in that direction and saw what appeared to be a toy dog slowly rising out of a box in the corner. "Rico, hurry up and get that cabinet open! We're about to be attacked!"

"By what?"

"A robotic dog."

Rico paused briefly in his picking of the padlock on the cabinet to glance over his shoulder. "Oookay!" He got busy on the padlock again.

"I'm going to get away from you to try to draw the thing toward me. It's pretty big...nearly the size of a German Shepherd."

"What's it got for armament?"

"Looks like teeth. The eyes are glowing red. Let's see if I can blind it with my flashlight." She took her hand off the beam that had been muting it so the full force of the light shone into the red eyes of the now slowly approaching robotic dog. It waved its head from side to side, the lights behind its eyes seemed to change color slightly and still it came, not fast, but relentlessly toward Roxy.

"Rico, it's coming toward me. How you doin' on the lock?"

"Got it!" He wrenched open the cabinet and shined his light up and down in the recesses of each shelf. The steel cabinet stood six feet tall and was bolted to the wall. There were half a dozen deep shelves inside, each about four feet wide by two feet deep. Some shelves had numerous sealed boxes, others had can-like containers with covers. "Shit. How do I find what I'm looking for? Too many boxes."

Roxy was dancing around the room keeping away from the 'dog' and keeping it away from Rico at the cabinet. "Make it fast, buddy. I'm running outa room here!"

On a whim Rico dropped to the floor and peered into the bottom shelf. Pushed all the way into the back of the shelf was a large box with an open top. He pulled it out and peered into it and nearly screamed. Lying on the unmarked computer chips in the bottom of the box was a large snake. It had a horn on its nose, a triangular head, and wavy stripes all down its back. It was not happy, having been awakened from its lethargic sleep. The remains of some sort of meal was in a bowl in the box next to a container of water. Rico was halfway across the room before he remembered the robotic dog and became aware of Roxy's nearly shouting at him.

"Rico, what the fuck?"

"Snake!"

"Shit!"

"I nearly did!"

"Now what?"

"Under the snake are the goddamned unmarked chips."

"Shit!"

"You said that already."

"Watch it!"

"Goddamned dog! Aargh!" Rico's pants leg got too close to the robot dog's teeth and with a snap they'd ripped the fabric, scratching Rico's leg in the process.

"Jeesus, we've gotta be quiet and get the hell outa here." Roxy poked the AI dog with a wooden chair leg. It bit on the leg and made serious dents.

"Oh fuck. Someone lives here. I hear 'em upstairs." Rico pointed at the ceiling.

The sounds of someone rousing themselves overhead were unmistakable.

"Gimme that chair!" said Rico. He took the chair to the cabinet, tipped over the box and dumped out the snake and several of the unmarked chips, sidestepped the still sluggish but deadly creature and grabbed two of the plastic-boxed chips. He also grabbed a couple of the other ones from the upper shelves at random, and said, "Let's go. No need to clean this up. They already know someone's here. Out now!"

Roxy kicked the metal dog in the butt as it was making for Rico's leg again and when the dog turned toward her she jumped over it and made a beeline for the door. Rico was just ahead of her. They hit the street running. Someone poked his head out the upstairs window of the factory and shouted something in Portuguese at them. Fortunately the street was dark so there was not much chance of their being identified. Still, Roxy and Rico kept their heads down as they ran for their car. As soon as they turned the corner at the end of the street they slowed to a walk and continued along back to the car holding hands like the lovers they were.

CHAPTER 16
Flight

Two days later Rico Morgan and Mary Teslin walked into the reception room of Fortune Technologies. They were dressed casually to mimic Rico's plan of exposing Farchex. Both had light jackets that concealed their guns, Mary with a Glock 9mm and Rico with his Daly Hi-Power 9mm. The receptionist, a youngish lady who appeared to be of Chinese origin, asked him in perfect English, "What may I do for you today, sir and madam?"

Rico replied, "My name is Boris Luftin, this is my friend Ginny Harumfer, and we'd like to see Mr. August Farchex. We didn't tell him we were coming, so this will be a surprise for him."

"Should I tell him your names?"

"Yes, absolutely!"

She picked up a phone, hit a button, and announced Rico and Mary as, "There's a Boris Luftin and Ginny Harumfer here to see you, sir." She listened to the response, hung up, and said, "He'll be right here, sir."

Rico switched on the recorder he had hidden in his jacket pocket and he and Mary sat down on a couch in the reception room. They heard August Farchex coming, and as he entered the room Farchex said, "Hey guys, you need some more bogus chips? How's the sailboat, Ginny?" And then he realized it was not August Farchex nor Ginny Harumfer to whom he was speaking.

"There's your proof of collusion," said Rico to Mary.

"Doesn't sound to me like they're enemies," replied Mary.

"Not hardly!" Rico agreed. "My simple plan worked."

"Like a charm!"

"Who the hell are you?" The fat little man was dressed casually, no suit, just a checkered, black-and-gray, light cotton shirt and blue jeans.

Rico answered, "We're your worst nightmare, buster. We've got you on collusion with Boris Luftin to destroy his company, accessory to murder, and bribery of an intelligence officer in Australia."

"What the hell?!" Some blustering sounds escaped his mouth, and then he tried to control himself. "I don't care what you think you have, get the hell out of my company!"

"I think we ought to call the police first, don't you, 'Ginny'? Let 'em know August here is wanted for murder in the 'States, bribery in Australia, and defrauding his customers here in Casablanca."

"I never murdered anyone! What the heck are you talking about? Who in blazes are you two? What gives you the right to accuse me of anything? Do you have any credentials? Arrest warrant? What goes, here?"

"My name is Rico Morgan and this is my friend Mary Teslin. We indeed have credentials. I was hired by Boris Luftin to find out why his computers are destroying his company and why his CEO was murdered. Mary here's with the CIA, investigating the bribe you sent to Miles Drapcox in Australia.

You admitted to conspiracy when you walked into the room. Luftin said you were his enemy, not his partner in conspiracy. In case you're wondering, I have a recording of your comments and a viable witness to them." Rico flashed his recorder. "Your bogus chips are installed in Luftin's robotics. How do I know that? Because we just got back from Portugal and brought along a bunch of your phony chips. Here's one of 'em. Note the lack of identification marks, just like the ones that cost Tesla Motors a ton of money when they failed on Elon's assembly line a few weeks ago. A scan of this chip revealed the installation of bogus data, scheduled to kick in after six hundred oscillations, give or take a hundred. Mr. Farchex, you're screwed."

"What makes you think my company made that chip? It's unmarked!"

"It came out from under the belly of a Lataste viper in your front office in Faro. There were many more chips there, all unmarked, just like this one."

"What's more," said Mary, we found the data in your books that proves payments of a total of forty thousand euros, to be converted to Australian dollars, were made to Miles Drapcox, head of ASIO in Canberra. The Australian authorities have been notified of this, as well as the Chinese company that was responsible for the construction of the factory you paid to have destroyed. As Mr. Morgan put it, you're screwed."

Farchex said, "I see," and then smiled. The frown on his face disappeared. He spoke over the shoulders of Rico and Mary and said, "Miss Yu, please keep these people here while I see to my business." Then he addressed the two. "Thank you for your time. I regret I must now take my leave. My secretary, Yu Sum Ting, will entertain you while I go back to work."

Mary looked over her shoulder and saw the AK-47 that the receptionist was now pointing at their backs. "Rico, don't move. She's got us covered."

Farchex slipped out of the room back the way he had come.

"He's running," said Rico.

"Yes. What's next?"

"Well, we'll have to stay here until Miss Yu puts down her big gun. By the way," Rico spoke softly so Yu Sum Ting would not hear, "I presume you have the means to track him by his cell phone?"

"Yes, assuming he carries one."

"We'll have to ask the lovely lady with the ugly gun to provide us with his cell number."

"You two shut up! Sit down there!"

Rico and Mary sat. "How long do we have to sit here, Miss Yu? Can't we just leave? By the way, do you know you're breaking the law?"

"You came in here and told me lies. So who's breaking the law, eh?" She pointed the gun low, aimed at the floor now.

"If you shoot us you're going to jail for the rest of your life. Or here in Morocco you might well lose your head, I don't know the local custom. What are you gonna do, Miss Yu? What if we just get up and walk out of here?"

"Sit where you are!" Up came the gun again.

Mary tried. "You know your employer, Mr. Farchex, is guilty of an international bribe. You heard us tell him what we've found. We were not making it up. He's a crook. Do you want to go down with him? He's corrupt. You're being used."

Yu's Chinese background started to kick in with all the stress she was in. "Mr. Farchex, he give good job, keep me and many bluthers and sisters off the street. Without him we have nothing! So we Chinese immigrants tly do good for him. Who care if he bad? Not me!"

"You might not care now, but once he's tracked down and in jail it will not go well with you." Rico tried to inform her. "Others know about this. Our partners, the local police, international police, all of them are closing in on him as we speak." Rico stood up. "The next knock on your door, the next person who comes into this office, might be the cops and when they see you with the gun they might just open fire. So please put the gun down and let us go."

The gun drooped, but Sum Ting held onto it. "I don't believe you! Mr. Faachex good man. Many of my countrymen work for him. All-ee Chinese-ee."

Suddenly the door opened, Sum Ting screamed and stared, terrified, at the person entering. In the blink of an eye Rico and Mary had their handguns out pointing at her. "*Don't move!*" Rico shouted at her, which held her attention long enough for Mary to jump across the room and grab the AK-47 out of Sum Ting's hands.

Rico turned his attention to the person who had just entered the room. It was the mail-delivery man, whose face was now quite white as a result of entering into the grand drama playing out in the reception room of the company. "Sorry, sir, we're just rehearsing for a play. Nothing to see here, so please put the letters on the desk and leave." Rico waved him towards the door, keeping his gun out of sight behind him.

The man did just that, but no one thought he was convinced by the explanation. He was a Moroccan native and actually had no idea what the English-speaking, crazy Americans were saying.

As soon as the mailman left Rico locked the entry door and he and Mary accosted Yu Sum Ting. "What's his cell phone number? Where is he going? Do you have any idea?"

"I say nothing. You two go to hell."

Mary was rifling through the receptionist's desk. There was an ancient Rolodex on the shelf behind the girl's desk. As a last resort Mary looked there, under F, and in short order said, "Got it!"

Rico was browsing the desktop computer, looking for contacts and also said, "Got it."

He read the number and Mary said, "That's it. Let's go!"

Before they left Rico pulled the mag from the AK and cleared the carbine's chamber – which had been empty – and, taking the magazine with them, they left the Fortune Technologies factory. Outside the door Rico tossed the mag into a trash container down the street as they trotted to their rental car.

"What's the fastest way to get onto him, Mary?"

Mary had her cell phone out and punched a number. "This is it," she said. "Roxy! We need you to track this cell phone number. Tell us where it's going. The number is Farchex's. Yes, he's on the run. We're at the car now. He got a head start. Are you still at the hotel? Great. Tell you later." She broke the connection.

In the car Rico asked, "I'm guessing you're able to track him because you brought some CIA gizmo here?"

"We had it delivered. Basically a computer program on a dedicated laptop. We had a tough time in Australia keeping track of the guy we were after, so asked for it when we were reassigned to Casablanca. The unit was flown here from the U.S. as we flew here from Canberra. Did we tell you, one whole day, twenty-four hours, on the friggin' airplane? Man, what a drag."

Mary's cell phone hummed. It was Roxy. Mary put her on speaker-phone. "He's heading northeast up a highway marked as P3330. Looks like he's heading toward a burg called Mohammedia. There's a port there. Maybe he's got a boat to escape on. But where'd he go in a boat?"

"Maybe he'll head up or down the coast," said Rico, "but that's a long way from his factory. He could've had a boat at Casablanca port. Are there any airports out where he's heading?"

"Er...lemme look," said Roxy. "Why would he go to an airport when his factory is already at one?"

"Mohammed V does not have anything but jet fuel. No 100 Low-Lead. That's airplane gas, by another name. So if he has a prop-driven plane he'd have to keep it at a different airport. I know that because I tried to rent a small plane out of Mohammed V. There ain't none there."

"Here's an airport...Ben Slimane. Pretty big." Roxy's voice lingered in the car.

Rico said, "We're on N9 now. Should we turn off anywhere?"

"Lemme see.... No, said Roxy. "You're heading for that seaport. If Farchex doesn't go to the seaport but goes to the airport you'll still have a straight shot at getting there if you stay on N9. He's taking a back route, less easy to be found, I'd guess. Crap! He turned onto R305. Highway R305. The one he was on was about to become a dirt road. He turned left on R305. He may still be heading for the same seaport or the airport."

Mary said, "I'm betting he's going to the airport. More places to get lost."

"I think you're right, Mary." Rico pushed the rental car still faster, but soon had to slow down. "Shit! I see why he took the outer route. Roxy, we're approaching some heavy traffic that'll slow us down a whole lot. You sure we can get there from here?"

"Okay, Rico, are you anywhere near Tit Mellil?" Roxy was monitoring a satellite image of the area.

"Just passing through it."

"Look for highway P3310. There's a roundabout there."

"I see 3309...Keep going?"

"No! Follow around the roundabout nearly three-quarters of the way. That gets you to P3310 and that'll take you to the A1 highway, which is a fast direct shot to that seaport. Take the second right at the next roundabout you come to. It's only about a quarter mile and you should be able to see it."

"We're there," said Rico. A minute later he said, "We're on A1 and we're flyin'! Thanks, Rox."

"In about thirteen miles you'll cross a river called Owed Nafukky and right after that is the cutoff for highway R313 to the right. You'll go through a toll booth, looks like, and then you'll get to R313. Take that to the east, or southeast, the way you're going. Your man Farchex just turned into the entrance to Ben Slimane airport. That R313 will take you right to the airport entry in about six or seven miles."

"Owed Nafukky?" Rico replied.

Mary giggled.

"I don't know how to pronounce it. Looks like what I said."

Some minutes passed as Rico drove the route described by Roxy. Mary had a map pulled up on her cell phone and, as best she could, monitored the instructions and the road map.

"We're through the toll booth. So, what do we do when we get to the airport? Rico asked. "Can you see where he went?"

Roxy came back on the speaker phone, "He's gone to a hangar over the right end of the airport. Can't tell, but the hangar seems to be open. You're still on R313? Okay, turn to the left when you hit the roundabout that takes you to the airport. You go three-quarters of the way around it and end up going northeast toward the airport. Hmmm. Interesting. There's a bank there, and near it is a pharmacy and cafe with the same name. Don't go to either one. It'll kill you. They're called El Matar. The Killing, in Spanish. But there's a big sports center on the other side of the road. Might be interesting."

"Roxy, stay on point!" said Mary.

"Sorry."

Rico asked, "What do you suppose all these buildings are? They look like apartments, and there's dozens of 'em."

Mary said, "I have no idea. I'm not from around here."

Roxy said, "The nearby town is pretty large. Maybe the folks who live near the airport prefer the sound of jet engines overhead to the grinding noise of the city. Okay, Rico, when you get to the next big roundabout that's nearly a mile down the airport road, take the first right, and then the second left. That gets you close to the hangar where the cell phone is."

"Got it," said Rico. "I'm turning right now...there's a gate here."

"Back up, head toward the terminal," said Roxy, "always bearing right...Oh shit! Your man is taxiing to the airstrip. Good God! He took off from the taxiway! He's in one heluva hurry."

"Can you follow him in the air?"

"Yes, even easier than on the ground. So far he's heading south."

"Could you tell what kind of airplane he flew?"

"Twin engine. Looked like a low-wing. Beech Baron maybe?"

"Okay, now I've gotta find a plane to follow him. Where am I gonna find a rental? Or a charter?"

"Why not find out where he's going first? Might be easier if you know how far you need to go to catch him," Roxy suggested.

"You might as well take it easy now," said Mary. 'We can track him all the way to Cape Town if need be."

The women offered good reasoning and Rico reluctantly agreed. "Good points. If he's going to South Africa I don't want to try going there in a rental 172. Damn Baron, if it's a Baron, has a range of over a thousand miles. Maybe close to fifteen hundred. He could be going anywhere. How in hell do you know what a Beech Baron is, Roxy? "

"My uncle has one. Lovely airplane. What are you going to do?"

"What say we head back to my hotel room and get some lunch, or dinner, and then see what gives with ol' August?"

Roxy said "See you there," and signed off.

Mary said, "Excellode!"

"What?"

"Good idea!"

"Let's go!" Rico wheeled the car around and headed at a more leisurely pace back to Casablanca.

CHAPTER 17
Planning

"*Fuck!*" Rico screamed. "The middle of nowhere!"

"Piss!" Roxy ejaculated.

"Good gravity!" Mary exclaimed. "Why there?!"

Back in the girls' hotel room Rico and Roxy and Mary all expressed disgust with the information displayed on the CIA's special tracking laptop. It showed the landing location of August Farchex.

"Why there, indeed. What can he be doing *there*? How in blazes am I going to get there?!" Rico asked.

"Charter? Can they refuel if you go there?" Roxy replied.

"It's twelve hundred miles from here," said Mary. But look, here's an international airport at Mopti, not too far away. Only 175 miles from there. So your charter can fly you in, and then fly to Mopti International and refuel, assuming there's no fuel at the airport where he drops you off. I guess you'll want the pilot to hang around while you're there? Otherwise you'll have to contact the charter outfit again and pay for four trips back and forth. That's forty-eight hundred miles."

"Fornicate with buffalo!" said Rico. I really don't want to go to Timbukfuckingtu!

"How else you gonna get this goon, my man?" This from Roxy. " 'Cause that's where he's at! ...Buffalo?"

"Is there any need for all of us to go? Or just me?" Rico paced the hotel room while ruining his normal hairdo with both his hands. His long hair stood up here and there, reflecting the craziness he felt at the info displayed that August Farchex had indeed fled to Timbuktu.

"We don't need to go," said Roxy. "We have all we need on the guy with the data from Yeats' hacking, which proved he sent the bribe to Australia."

"Aren't you guys supposed to bring this jerk to justice?" Rico was pissed at the world.

"I guess we could do that, sure," said Mary. "Or we can sit here in Casablanca. Maybe visit Rick's Cafe again. Rico can go get this guy and bring him home to us here, eh, Roxy?"

"Sounds like the plan. So, what should we have for dinner over there?" Roxy grinned at Mary behind Rico's back.

"How am I even going to find him once I'm there?" Rico finger-combed his hair back to approximately where it belonged. "He could sit on a rooftop with a sniper rifle and pick me off. I understand there's lots of terrorist activity throughout Mali. The U.S. government doesn't want anyone to go there. If I got shot, no one in Timbuktu would care. So maybe I should just go home and let you guys sort this out."

"He'll know you're there the second you land. Not that many people fly to Timbuktu, so any aircraft landing there so soon after he did will be watched by him, or by any goons he may have there working for him." Roxy started pacing the room too. "Might be better to land at Mapco, or whatever it's called, and drive to Timbuktu."

"Or not!" exclaimed Rico. "If an airplane spooks him, imagine how a car pulling into town from Mopti would spook him even more. And a car's easier to watch. Can I even rent a car at Mopti?"

Mary suggested, "You could parachute down at night."

"Aargh!" Rico attacked his hair again.

Rico took the two ladies to La Bavaroise, the French restaurant he'd eaten at a few days before. The dinner was marvelous, as was the wine. The conversation was a bit on the dreary side, however.

"Timbuktu. Fuck. Shit. Piss. Good wine, eh?" Rico sipped the Moroccan Beaujolais.

"Great wine. Great choice of restaurant," replied Roxy. "How's the beef?"

"Superb! How's the fish?"

"Fabulous, said Mary."

"Yummy," said Roxy. "Never had better."

Rico had a beef filet medallion with a side of salad and another of french fries in a small deep-fry dish, the whole served on a plank instead of a plate, the salad with three types of dressing. The ladies had fish, grilled fillets stacked up with some greenery and carrots, and they split a bottle of Moroccan white wine, recommended by the waiter, between them.

"Thank you for bringing us here, Rico. How'd you find this place?"

"Well, Mary, I used my skills at restaurant hunting the night I got here. I rejected a fishy-sounding poisonous place, turned down a laundromat, and came here."

"Pure luck, then," said Mary.

"Yes indeed. Works every time. So, who's going to Timbuktu with me?"

Roxy looked at Mary, Mary nodded, Roxy grimaced, and said, "Hate to tell you this. We both are. Our orders came through to find out exactly what this guy is doing in Timbuktu. So you'll have our company."

"Well! That's better! In fact that's great, and it calls for a treat." Rico called the waiter over with a wave and spoke quietly to him so the two women would not hear. In short order the waiter brought a delightful array of desserts, including fruits, chocolates, berries, the works, and a small bottle of Cointreau.

"Yay Rico!" said Mary.

Roxy grabbed the bottle of Cointreau.

After dinner, Roxy caught a glimpse of the check, which Rico paid. It was over 1200...somethings. "Good God," she said. "What's that in real money?"

"None of your business," replied Rico. "That's neither dollars nor euros, so don't worry."

"We're on government funds," said Mary.

"I'm on Luftin's funds," said Rico, "so I wish it was more!"

"Come on," said Roxy. "What is it really?"

"Dirhams are about a tenth of U.S. dollars. So, call it a hundred and twenty bucks. Damned cheap, really, for what we got."

"It can't be that cheap. You sure?" Mary couldn't believe it. "Not for that quality and service."

"That's it, kids. Remember what I said about luck!"

"Wow!" Roxy said. Then, in her best Schwarzenegger voice, "I'll be back!"

The three were walking back to their hotels, which were essentially next door to each other, when it happened. The trio walked from the restaurant west on Boulevard Ben Abdellah for half a block, turned north on Rue Chaouia for another short block and then turned west again onto Rue Leon l'Africain, which street led to Rico's hotel, the Odyssee Center, and then the street name changed for some unknown reason – though continuing in the same direction – to Rue M Kamal, which led to the Oum Palace where the two women were staying. The three friends had walked maybe fifty yards west on Rue Leon l'Africain when a car with no headlights came roaring around the corner behind them, out of the north extension of Rue Chaouia, and continued up the street in their direction. Roxy looked back at it and recognized it for what it was. She saw the gun sticking out the window of the rear seat of the car, and that was what saved them.

"*Get down now!*" she shouted at the top of her lungs, and tackled Mary to the ground at the same time the burst of fully automatic gunfire came from the car. Rico dived to the ground near a parked car, rolled into the gutter, and came up on one knee with his gun out, but the car turned left at the corner and was instantly out of sight.

"How'd they find out who we are?" Rico asked, after they got up, hotfooted it to his hotel, and went to his room.

Roxy was doctoring Mary's and her own cuts and scrapes as best she could with some hydrogen peroxide to wash the street dirt out. Mary had a bad cut on her arm where she hit the edge of the curb when Roxy tackled her. Roxy's knees were both skinned. Rico had a banged-up elbow and a tear in his jacket. All their bruises would show later.

"And *where* we are, too," replied Roxy.

"Wow!" said Mary. A real drive-by shooting!"

"It ain't no joke no more, Mary dearest," said Roxy. "Look here." She pointed out a bullet hole in Mary's skirt. Mary turned white and the smile disappeared from her face.

"Okay," said Rico. "The only one who knew where we were, at least knew where I was, is Yeats in Boise. I have not contacted him in a week or so. Farchex would have had time in flight to contact Boris Luftin in Atlanta and find out who I was exactly, but he still would not have been able to know where I was, much less where I was going to eat dinner tonight."

Mary asked, "How did you choose this hotel?"

"Er...it was recommended by...*SHIT*! By Luftin! He said he'd never been here but his people had, and they liked this place fine. So flying fatty Farchex in his fast fucking airplane calls Luftin, says the jig's up, and where can his goons in Casablanca find Rico Morgan so they can stop him? Gets the hotel info, sends someone to look up the room number, and...."

"*Double shit!*" said Roxy in a near whisper. She pulled Rico and Mary into the bathroom, closed the door and turned on the water. Then she explained. "The room service girl was Chinese! Or looked like one, anyway, when we all got here yesterday and she was cleaning the room. She put a bug in there."

"Damn! You're right," said Rico. "If we leave it alone maybe we can feed them false information."

"Yes," replied Roxy, "if we haven't blown it already with our discussion."

"We can but try," said Rico. "Let's find out if there is a bug here first. While we look, we can talk about how hard it's going to be to find Farchex. I don't recall telling the bug we know where he is, did we?"

"No," said Roxy. "You recall, Mary?"

"No mention of where he went, but we did say we knew he was on an airplane."

"Crap. You're right." Rico went for his hair again. "At any rate, let's leave Timbuktu and rental airplanes out of our talk."

"Got it," said Mary.

Roxy nodded. "Let's go see if we can find it."

Mary found it under the lampshade by the bed, near the land-line phone.

Rico said, "Well, the bastard got away. So we're screwed and he's free. Let's go get a drink."

The three left the room and went to Roxy and Mary's room in the Oum Palace hotel just down the street. No one threatened them along the way, and they were able to continue their discussion of the proposed flight to Timbuktu.

"We'll have to do all our planning outside my room," said Rico. "I'll have to contact the charter guy from here, too. I guess it's too late to do it tonight."

"Do you want to sleep here on the couch tonight, Rico?" asked Roxy.

"Might be a good idea," said Mary, "because if they know where your room is and want to stop you they might make a direct attack."

"Or I could go there and hope they try, and maybe find out more about all this. But you're right, I might fall asleep, and of course they might not come, so I'll lose a night's rest for nothing. Okay, the couch it is. Some sleep's better than none. But first I have to go back there and get some stuff."

They all had a drink from a bottle of Bols Genever gin Roxy had in the room.

Rico returned to his hotel room, and when he opened the door there were two Chinese cleaning girls there, and they looked so much alike they could have been sisters. They appeared to be in their mid-twenties.

"Hi, ladies," said Rico.

"Hello, kind sil, we just clean up youl loom a bit," one said. She smiled at him, and caught his eye. The second girl, who was behind him, stuck her hand in her pocket and pulled out a sap. Rico watched her in the mirror out of the corner of his eye and when she took a step closer to him he stepped to the side, whirled, grabbed her arm and flung her to the ground, stunning her. The first girl, now behind Rico, yelled and threw a kick at his head. He ducked and took the blow on his shoulder. Rico stepped back to get his balance, spun and replied with a kick of his own, a roundhouse like Chuck Norris is famous for. Rico aimed for her face, but the girl partly ducked and his kick caught her on the shoulder, knocking her down next to the other girl.

Rico had his gun out in an instant and said, "Stay down! Don't move!" This stopped both girls in their tracks, both still on the floor. "You!" Rico pointed at the first girl. "What's your name?"

The girl said, "Yu Bang Mi."

"Fat chance, bitch!" He looked at the other one and repeated his question. "What's your name?"

The second girl replied, "Yu Mi Tu."

"Smart asses, eh? Who sent you? Was it Farchex?"

"Yu Sum Ting," said the first girl.

"More smart answers, eh? Well...."

"No!" the second girl replied in perfect English. "Those are our names. Our sister, Yu Sum Ting, is the receptionist at the Farchex factory."

"Shit!, said Rico. "I remember, now. So you're Mi Tu and your sister is indeed Bang Mi. Okay, so...did Sum Ting send you, or was is August Farchex?"

"Sum Ting like that." She smiled.

"Crap!" Rico realized he wasn't going to get anywhere with the two. "Get outa here, both of you, and don't come back. Now!"

When the girls were gone Rico locked and chained the door and looked for the bug. It was gone.

The charter was easy to set up. Rico got on the phone the next day to the same outfit that took them to Faro in the Cessna Citation M2 jet. When asked about refueling, the pilot said, "Yes, they have A1 jet fuel in Timbuktu. So, no problems there. If I stay there and wait for you it'll cost you for my room and board, plus a stipend for each day there, but that's cheaper than flying back and forth twice. How long do you figure to be in that tiny town?"

Rico answered. "Hopefully only a day or two. Might stretch to several days, max of a week. That any problem for you?"

"Not at all. We don't have a lot of clients right now, so whatever you need to do is okay by us. May I ask what you're doing there?"

"We're U.S. law-enforcement people, " said Rico. "There's a man there we need to apprehend and bring back. He's wanted for murder and coercion in the U.S., and bribery in Australia. The Aussies gave us an international arrest warrant to bring him to the U.S., which might seem strange, but that's how it goes. There are two law-enforcement outfits involved, me and the U. S. government. I have priority because I'm after him for murder. The two ladies who will travel with me want him for the bribery charge. Do you have any problems with that?"

"Not as long as he's restrained enroute," said the pilot.

Roxy held out a note to Rico. She wanted to know his name.

"What's your name?" asked Rico.

"I'm Apeez Uvrok."

"Got it. See you tomorrow at ten in the morning."

CHAPTER 18
Timbuktu

The rest of the day before the flight to Timbuktu the three were still all together in the girls' hotel room in Casablanca. They planned what they would do once they got there, and also discussed in detail what they needed to take along. Their research told them there were half a dozen hotels in Timbuktu, a surprise to them all.

"What's the population?" Mary asked.

"I see here," said Rico, looking at a computer screen, "it's about thirty-five thousand people, down from fifty thou about ten years ago. So they've lost fifteen hundred people a year over the last decade. I suppose there's not much to do in that burg. Tourism support, entertainment for the terrorists, the usual suspects. I also see here back in 1450 this was an important city in the scheme of things. Population then was a hundred thousand. That would have made it one of the more important cities in the world at that time. What was the population of New York City, or San Francisco back then? *Zero!* They didn't exist."

"A hundred thousand!" exclaimed Roxy. "Even thirty thousand today? I'd never believe it from aerial photos of the town. So it has hotels, then...good! At least we don't have to carry camping gear and food in there, like I was thinking we would. But we damn well better carry our guns."

"Amen," said Rico and Mary together.

"Do we need rifles? Shotguns?" Mary asked.

"Doubtful," said Rico. "They're never carried when needed, and in the way all the time when they are. Vests would be a good idea, even though it's hotter'n blazes there."

"Okay," said Mary. "But lots of ammo, eh? We've all got nines."

Rico laid out the task. "First we've got to locate our man. That'll be tough, I'm afraid."

"What about our satellite cell-phone tracker?" asked Roxy. "Did you forget about it?"

"Actually I did. Will it work there?"

"Yes," Roxy replied. "As long as his phone's charged and close to him, then we oughta be able to find him. He may've got onto our tracking by now, though. Especially if we show up there and he thought he'd escaped. And we don't know what the cleaning girls told him."

"If Farchex went there to jump into a hole and hide," said Rico, "that means he has agents or support personnel in Timbuktu that he can trust. He won't be without eyes on us, that's for sure. We won't know anyone there who can help us, except by shit luck."

"Whatta you mean?" asked Mary.

Roxy explained. "If someone doesn't like Farchex and wants him gone, that person might be able to help us."

"Right," replied Rico. "Whether or not we find an ally we've gotta be on guard twenty-four-seven. For all we know, the whole town loves this guy and wants to protect him. It'd be a good idea to post a guard at night, and we oughta stay in one room if that's possible. At any rate, this isn't gonna be a piece of cake."

"I think we can count on that," replied Roxy.

"What the hell," said Mary. "I've survived one drive-by shooting. Bring it on!"

"There's absolutely *nothing* down there! All sand and more sand and nothing else whatsoever, for as far as I can see. And we're twenty thousand feet up, so I can see pretty far!" Roxy peered out the windows on both sides of the charter jet, and sat down in disgust.

"Not quite true," said Rico. "About halfway to Timbuktu there's a salt-mining place called Taoudenni, still in operation, and it's been in operation over a hundred years. Maybe longer. The settlement has been there over four hundred years. The salt, well, the area used to be a salt lake, so it's been there a long time. There used to be a prison there, at Taoudenni. The inmates, generally political prisoners of one or another side of the ruling spectrum, used to work digging salt out of the desert. Those big salt blocks are carried to Timbuktu, the closest town, by means of camel trains. I say 'are' because the salt mining's still going on, though there are no prisoners involved...probably. Taoudenni's about four hundred miles north of Timbuktu, with nothin' but the Sahara in between. No! That's not right! There's a little burg there, almost abandoned today, that used to be a stopping place for the camel trains.

"Remember the old jokes about going to work in the salt mines? That wasn't really a joke. Lots of the poor bastards confined in the prison died there. I read there's over a hundred graves at the mine, and only about a dozen have someone's name on 'em. Today only the blowin' sand keeps 'em company.

"There's a road out of Timbuktu that goes to Taoudenni, but I doubt it's useable. I'd guess sandstorms would blow it away, cover it to uselessness. I also read they use trucks these days to haul the salt, but from what I've seen of the terrain, and satellite images of the old road, I'd guess a camel's a better proposition."

Mary said, "I'd walk a mile for a Camel."

"Ah!" said Rico. "You remember the old ad. Remember the billboards with some guy's mug on 'em...Meet the Turk!"

Roxy said, "And now let's have a moment of silence for Joe Camel, killed by the tobacco company that invented that sorry piece of crap. Or we could laugh our asses off at the fools who fell for that."

"Ah," said Rico, "but they were kids! Back in his day, Joe Camel, the 'smooth character,' was more readily identified by young people than Mickey Mouse."

"Rico, you smoke cigars. How can you condemn cigarette smokers?" asked Mary.

"Actually I don't condemn them, but I wouldn't touch a cigarette, let alone smoke one. Darlin', if you don't know the difference, here it is in a nutshell. Cigarettes are full of chemicals. Over a hundred of 'em in some cases. Cigars have none. Zero. Zip. Nada. If that doesn't tell you the difference, look at George Burns. He smoked cigars all his life from age fourteen. It was estimated he smoked around 300,000 cigars during his lifetime – but only four a day in his later years. It takes me two days to smoke one big cigar. Burns lived to be over a hundred years old. The recently deceased Richard Overton died in a hospital at age one hundred and twelve. Overton smoked a dozen cigars a day, and drank whiskey, too."

"But didn't Rush Limbaugh smoke cigars? He was recently found to have cancer."

"After many years of smoking cigarettes, yes. Don't forget, the tobacco industry got the blame for all the open-atmospheric atom-bomb testing from 1945 to 1963. It continued in France 'til 1974 and in China until 1980. The open-atmosphere nuclear blasts out in Nevada in the early 1950s killed more people in the U.S. from persistent radiation than all the cigarette deaths combined, but no one tells you that. Except me. Before the second world war everybody smoked in the U.S. and no one got lung cancer. Do the math."

"Who wants a drink?" Apeez, the pilot, stuck his head through the open cockpit door.

"Yay!" said Mary. "All this tobacco talk makes me want a cigarette, and I don't smoke."

"Check out that cooler there, and there's glasses up here in this closet, too."

"How much longer, Apeez?" Roxy asked.

"About two more hours. The flight is three hours and a bit overall, and we've been up here an hour. In about another hour we'll be over the salt mine. You might see some of the ruins, even at this altitude."

When Apeez went back to the pilot's seat Rico, who was a pilot, commented on the upcoming airport. "Oddly," he said, "there's no taxiway at the Timbuktu airport. Here's a quiz, ladies. There are two ways to land, runway 07 or runway 25. They're of course the same strip of tarmac. The airport terminal is at the eastern end, which is near the start of the 25 end of the strip. These numbers are simply degrees on a compass. The one called 07 is at 70 degrees, or east-northeast, and the other end obviously points 180 degrees the other way, or 250 degrees. It's runway 25. So, why is there no taxiway? Anyone?"

Roxy said, "Duhh?"

Mary said, "Also duhh?"

Rico continued his pilot-bragging dissertation. "This is a desert strip. If there's a wind, any significant wind at all, there's gonna be a dust storm. In a dust storm no one is going to land at Timbuktu. They'll divert to Mopti or elsewhere. If there's no wind, everyone comes into runway 07 which leads directly to the terminal. Outbound, again with no wind, they can take off on 25 going the other way. Hence there's really no need for a taxiway. In the odd circumstance of a light tailwind without lots of dust, such a condition might make 07 unusable. Then the airplane can land on 25 and turn around and taxi back to the terminal on the main strip. Anywhere in the world there's significant air traffic that wouldn't work, but out here it's a charm that saved lots of unnecessary costs and cleaning efforts after any dust gets blown onto the strip and the taxiway, if it had one."

The rest of the flight went without incident, and without Rico lighting up a stogie. The jet set down on runway 07 in the early afternoon on the Timbuktu runway, taxied to the end of the runway, turned right and rolled to a stop near the terminal and refueling pumps, and that is where the three friends got out, with their light suitcases in tow.

As soon as they were on the tarmac Rico said, "Where's the airplane this bozo flew down here?"

It was nowhere to be seen.

"Are we sure this guy's still here?"

"He was," said Roxy, "half an hour ago. I checked while we were in the air. I got a satellite feed on his phone in the area of the city, to the north of the airport.

"Let me ask at the terminal," said Rico. "See if you can find us a taxi. I won't be long.

Rico entered the recently rebuilt and very attractive terminal, went to a counter and asked for someone who spoke

English. A girl behind the counter said she did, so Rico asked her, "A day or two ago a twin-engine airplane flew in here. My friends and I are friends of the owner. Do you know where the airplane went? Is the owner still in the area?"

"Yes, you must mean Mr. French. He put his airplane in one of the rental hangars at the central area of the airport. He's still in town, I'm sure."

"Do you know where he's staying?"

"No, I'm sorry. The hangars are self-serving. There's no one there when you put your airplane in. It's generally arranged as the pilot flies in here. He talks to the tower who tells him where he can taxi to store the aircraft. The pilot puts his airplane in the hangar, and then when he comes back to the airport to get his airplane and fly away, the pilot pays the rental fee to collect his airplane. No one is at the hangar except a helper boy, so no one would know where the airplane owner is staying. All he does is leave his phone number."

"We've already got that, so thank you."

Rico rejoined the two women and told them the good news.

They looked for a rental car, but there were none. A sort-of taxi was at the edge of the tarmac and Mary, who spoke a little French, asked if they could get a ride to their hotel, the Hotel du Desert. Because the taxi didn't have a meter Mary knew enough to verify the cost before they all got in and were on the way to the hotel.

On the way, Mary asked, "Why this hotel?

Rico answered, "It's close to the UN fort and it's not too far into the center of the city. In fact it's near the southwestern edge of the city. It's not far from the canal, and also a short ride from the airport. Because we don't know where our quarry is, I figured it'd be okay to start there, you know, barely into the city. The hotel has two stories, so we can get up in the air a bit to see what's what, have a look around. It looked good tactically to me, put it that way."

"Does it have a bar or restaurant?" Roxy asked.

"It does serve food. Also there's another restaurant close by, the hospital isn't far, and there's a bank near it as well."

The cab took them to the Hotel du Desert, and as they unloaded their plunder the cabbie said something in French to Mary. It clearly got her attention, and when they had moved into their adjoining two rooms, she said, "The cabbie said to beware the red-eyed monster at night. I asked him what it was and he just said, 'Beware!' So what's that all about?"

Rico suggested, "Maybe we can ask the people here at the hotel. It might mean something to them. Meantime I suggest we take a walk around and get the lay of the land."

"Looking for a hooker, Rico?" Roxy asked.

"Eh?"

"The *lay* of the land...."

"Good grief!"

CHAPTER 19
On the Town

The gang of three walked towards the northeast of Timbuktu, out to the main drag, up and down a few side streets, and quickly discovered there was a whole lot of desert and not much else in Timbuktu. There was a soccer field not far from their hotel, but no one was using it except for a few kids kicking a ball around. Wind-blown dust was everywhere. In a desert storm, they figured, all you could do was remain indoors and hope the sand didn't cover your house. The whole town had a distinctly brown and dirty look to it. The buildings appeared to be made of mud blocks.

Rico thought it would be a good idea to talk with the United Nations people before Rico and the girls started shooting up the town. The girls agreed. Accordingly, they all walked up the stone-laid streets and turned this and that corner until they arrived at the United Nations fort. They took with them Rico's International Arrest Warrant, basically a letter of authority from the Atlanta PD, and the girls' papers from the U.S. government in Washington, DC, and Australia, all of which clearly established their combined need and authority to apprehend one August Farchex for murder and mayhem.

Mary, with her bit of French, took charge. "Gentlemen, we'd like to let your headman here know that we are law enforcement officers from the United States, and we are in Timbuktu to arrest someone who has broken laws in Morocco, Australia, and in the United States. Can you direct us to the proper person here?"

The man answered in reasonable English, "The person you want is me. My name is Aziz Arnot, and I control the law enforcement in Timbuktu. Of course there is also the local police, but in these times of terrorism they can't do much against the oppressors. Who is the person you are after?"

Mary replied, "He is named August Farchex. He may be using an alias of Mr. French." She showed the man a photo the CIA had acquired from the Morocco police, a few years old, from the man's business licence in Casablanca. Have you heard of him?"

"No, madam, I have not," answered Aziz. "How do you plan to proceed?"

"We intend to find him first, which might be a difficult task. About all we can do is walk about and ask people if they know who he is." By previous agreement of them all, Mary didn't mention the CIA satellite tracker. She continued. "It ought not to be difficult for us to find him. He flew in here in an expensive twin-engine airplane, and someone ought to know where to look for its owner."

"Did you ask at the airport?"

"Yes, we did, but it was no help."

"There are only a few hotels in town. You might telephone them and ask if your man is staying there. Other than that, your papers seem to be in order and I wish you luck, but please keep us informed of your progress."

As they were leaving, Mary asked the man, "Have you heard about something terrorizing the local residents in the late-night hours? We were led to believe something here might be frightening them."

"There have been some silly rumours, but don't worry yourselves about it. If you see something, let us know and we'll see what we can do."

"Thank you."

The trio took their leave.

"Well," said Rico, "as it's close to dinnertime we could head back to the hotel and try their evening cuisine, or we could try one of the local restaurants. Any suggestions?"

Roxy replied, "Let's eat out, as long as we're out. Where do we go?"

Mary said, "I have a map on my phone that indicates there's a bistro up that street over there. Shall we go see?" They began following Mary's map.

On the way to the restaurant they encountered some young people kicking a soccer ball around. One of them said to them, "Hello, Americans!"

The three friends stopped, and Rico asked, "My friend, you speak English!"

The youth, perhaps fifteen years old, came over to them and replied, "I have a bit of English."

"Can you tell us anything about a red-eyed monster? We heard it roams around here at night."

"Oh, yes, a horrible thing. Do not go near it! It hurt my friend over there. See, he has only four fingers! He lost a finger to it!"

"A finger?! What happened?" asked Roxy.

"Yes! A finger! He got close to it and tried to kick it and it grabbed his hand and broke off one of his fingers. It wouldn't let go and he pulled and his finger got left behind."

"That's horrible!" replied Roxy. "What did it look like? How big? What color?"

"Almost as tall as him!" He pointed to Rico. "More paint and shiny metal than clothes. It had a squarish head. Antennas on top. Two red eyes. No ears. A grille for a mouth...like a radio speaker. It had some big plates in front, like a vest. Its legs looked almost normal, almost human. The hand had only four fingers! It didn't wear any shoes. It looks like a man with red eyes!"

"Rico," Roxy said, "it's a friggin' robot!"

"Well shit!" said Rico. "Who do we know who makes robots around here? Thank you!" he said to the boy. "Here's something for you and your friend. Buy him some ice cream or something with it."

The boy ran off and rejoined his friends, and they saw him give the money to his wounded friend.

"That was gruesome," said Mary. "Poor bastard. There goes my appetite."

The trio continued on their way and soon were at the Pâtisserie Aco. In short order Mary regained her appetite. The evening meal was more than suitable to all of them, particularly the pastries made at the restaurant. The cost, bearing in mind the remoteness of the area and the fact that most of all the edible things had to be flown in, was reasonable.

After dinner Rico complimented the owner on the high quality of the food, the pastries and the service, then asked the proprietor, "Kind sir, we wonder if you know anything at all about someone named August Farchex, or perhaps another fellow called Mr. French? We are friends of theirs and would like to pay them a visit. We understand one or the other of them is in town now."

"I have not heard those names. Can I ask, what do they look like?"

Mary brought out the photograph again. The restaurant owner gave a short gasp, but stopped himself instantly. "No, I have never seen this man. Sorry."

Unfortunately for the restaurant owner all three of the friends had seen and heard his short gasp.

"Come on, man," said Rico. He held out a sizeable chunk of the local money as a 'tip' and asked again. "Are you sure you've never seen him?"

"Well," the owner hesitated, licked his lips, glanced right and left, and pocketed the extra-large 'tip.' "Mr. French, you say? Well, you might look at an old store, now shut down. It's in the east-central portion of town. It used to be called the Fortune Teller, and the old sign is still up there." He gave rough directions how to find it based on some Timbuktu landmarks. Then he added, "I'm sorry you didn't like your meal, and please don't come back."

The three took their leave.

"My friends," said Rico as they left the restaurant, "Timbuktu is about two and a half miles, north to south, and just over two miles wide. That means our man is within five square miles. The tallest building I've seen here is, what, four stories tall, so there's not a lot of hiding places. Is this 'old store' our best bet?"

Mary said it. "Our best bet is to go back to our hotel and see what our little cell-phone finder tells us. It works by satellite, so if he's here we can at least point a solid finger at him before we go hunting for shut-down stores."

By the time they got to the hotel it was getting dark. The attractions of the town, surprising to them all, held their interest in their casual wandering on the way back to their hotel. Their walk in the cooling evening air was a pleasant change from the heat of the day, so they were in no hurry to get inside the hotel, even though it was air conditioned.

The ladies were about to bid good night to Rico when he asked, "Can you at least give it a look to verify our man is still in town and has not smashed his cell phone?" Rico was impatient, despite the relaxed atmosphere of the sleepy town.

"Okay. Come on in and Mary'll set it up."

In short order the CIA laptop was up and running, and to their satisfaction a red dot appeared in the east-central portion of the town, where the proprietor of the restaurant had indicated the disused shop was.

Early the next day Rico told the women he was going to walk to the area where the so-called shut-down store was, to get a feeling for the place and see if he could learn anything. "I think it'll be a good idea to go either alone or with only one of you. I think we all need to see it, but not as a group. In fact, so far as Farchex knows, based on our one face-to-face in his outer office the day he fled, I'm in it with Mary. So he ought not to see us together."

"You could wear a disguise," suggested Roxy. "In fact we all could put on robes, masks on our faces, towels on our heads and pass as locals, and then get a look at the place. And if he's used to seeing two, why not give him three?"

And so they did. Rico and the two women, in their hasty disguises, easily found the building that had been indicated by the reluctant restaurant owner. It had been a store in days long past, and a faded sign with 'Fortune Teller' on it sat forlornly against the front wall. The building was made in two stories, with a sort of shed built on top making a third place, or hidey-hole. Off to the side was a railed flat roof that could be a good place to get a tan, or a good place to set up a sniper's nest. The front door seemed to be boarded up as were the windows, even the tiny ones on the second floor. One odd thing was a sort of tower made of steel, like a radio-antenna support, on the roof. It rose twenty feet above the roof of the little shed on top. There was a look of age about the place, though that was a common look throughout ancient Timbuktu. More critical to this building was the feeling of a lack of life that seemed to permeate the building. The kids in the street were loath to play their games anywhere near it. One thing it did have, they noticed, was the evidence of footprints leading up to the boarded-up front door. Some looked new. There were also some piles of sand in the front that looked like they needed to be hauled away.

"Someone's been digging," said Roxy. "Maybe a basement?"

The trio walked around the block to get a look at the place from the back. There was another building in ruins on the same lot, and a wire fence that discouraged access from that side. They walked on. Mary had the foresight to take several photos of the place. On the way back home the trio remarked on several landmarks that might help them find the way in the dead of night, which is when Rico planned to visit it.

"If all's well this palooka doesn't know we're in town," he said. "Of course all seldom goes well, so he probably had a tracker on that airplane and knows we're in his neighborhood at this moment. Any of you carrying a phone?"

"Negative."

"Yes," said Mary. "I used it to take the photos. He'd have to know my number to find us, though. We have the latest technology in tracking and it's not available for him to buy."

"Good to know." Rico stopped. "So if I go there tonight, what am I gonna do? Break in and look around? To what benefit?"

"We could just go and knock on the door, see if he's in. If so, we arrest him." Roxy was thoughtful. "If he's there he might start shooting. And if he's there we really need to know why. I mean, what's he got here that he doesn't have in Casablanca?"

"Sand," said Mary. "And a certain amount of fear instilled in the locals, judging by that restaurant guy. He was spooked, that's for sure."

"We'd really like to know why he came here," said Roxy. "He's out of the grasp of Moroccan police, but heck, the Chinese can follow him here if they have a grudge. Though that can be damped a bit by the fact he hired so many Chinese at his factory. The only others who might want him would be the Aussies."

"If he didn't commit – or have committed – the murder, then he doesn't really have much to fear from the Americans," said Rico. "Collusion to defraud a company isn't all that big a deal compared to murder. So I, too, don't know why he came here. Unless just to get away from Morocco and us. Maybe he has something set up here that gives him protection? Any ideas?"

"Ary any," Roxy said. "That means no."

"I knew that. Mary?"

"As I said, sand. Seriously, can he do anything with all this sand that would give him protection? Create a sandstorm and blow it in our eyes?"

"Highly unlikely and Haile Selassie." Rico felt stupid and said so in that manner. "I'm going to my room and get a short nap. If you hear anything during the night it might be me, or it might be a burglar. Stay safe. See y'all in the morning."

CHAPTER 20
The Chase

It was near two in the morning when Rico was roused by his alarm. With a curse he got up, dressed in black, darkened his face and hands with a washable dye, put a light black jacket over his black tee shirt and stuck his Daly Hi-Power into the Bachman Slide holster at his side. A spare magazine rode on the opposite side, giving him twenty-seven rounds total, with one in the chamber. The ammo was 147-grain Federal Hydra-Shok hollowpoints. He also packed his usual pocket knife, which was an ancient Schrade Old Timer with one razor-sharp locking blade of three-inch length. He had a small flashlight and a lock-pick set. No crowbar.

He quietly made his way out of the hotel and began his march to the ancient shut-down store in mid-town. But for a faint house light or two the old town was dark. There was a sliver of a moon, and together with the stars it gave enough light to keep the private eye from running into things. Rico stopped fifty yards from the old store, put himself deep in the shadows, sat down, and proceeded to watch the store for tell-tale lights. After fifteen minutes he moved to another hide, just past the building, and did it again. He saw no lights, heard no activity. The soft bleat of a goat came from far off in the night. No one else was stirring. A slight breeze gently moved the tops of the few trees near the road. It was time to approach the building.

Rico kept to the shadows and decided to attack the right side of the building as he looked at it. There was an old wall that blocked the left side. A ladder was propped against the wall and Rico was tempted, but the right side had a sort of alley that let him get off the street and also keep him in shadow. He made his way down the side of the building, always listening for any sounds from the building. He kept looking up at the flat roof overhead and hoped no one was sleeping outdoors up there.

Near the side of the building grew a stout-looking tree. Rico decided to chance climbing it. Very slowly and as quietly as he could he ascended the tree until he could peer over the edge of the roof. No one was there. From his precarious perch in the tree he could not get onto the roof, so he went back down, again as quietly as he could. Once on the ground again he snuck alongside the building until he could peer around the back corner. No one was there. All was quiet. Shadows everywhere made the darkness darker. A lone door stood in the back wall.

Rico tried the back door and found it locked. He brought out his lock-pick set and quickly had the door open. He pushed it inward very slowly and shined his light into the room. No one was there, so he entered. Shining his light around the room he saw nothing but a few empty boxes and the remains of some wood crates. He heard a slight hum coming from beneath the wood floor. The hum was low, like the soft hum of a fluorescent lamp, and had been inaudible outside the building.

There were two doors in the room. One led to the front of the building. He peered in there and saw the backs of the boarded-up front door and windows. A flight of stairs led to the upper story. He gently closed the door and quietly approached the second door. It was built into a sturdy extension of the building against the right wall and could have been a closet, or a staircase going downward. Should he open it? He tried the handle and found it to be locked. There was no recognizable keyhole to pick, but an odd-shaped hole in the center of the door might have been some sort of locking or unlocking means, if one had the right 'key,' or odd-shaped device to make it work. Rico wondered if August Farchex might be in there.

"Let's take a look on the roof," he said to himself. Rico slowly climbed the staircase in the front room, keeping well to the outside wall to avoid creaking steps. One step made a slight downward motion but no sound. What Rico didn't know was that step was attached to a microswitch that set certain things in motion.

At the top of the stairs was an unlocked door that led out onto the deck, one story off the ground. This was the area that Rico thought would make a good sniper's shooting point. On the deck were two chairs and a small table that would do for an outdoor lunch or even a dinner.

Off the deck was another door that led into the enclosed part of this second story of the building. Rico picked the lock of the door leading into the room. It was empty. Another stair in there led to a trapdoor in the roof, above which Rico found the little shed from which the antenna protruded. It had a simple door with no lock. Rico opened it cautiously and saw an electronic box that looked like it could be an amplifier of some sort. It had small red and green bulbs on top. Both were lit up. Wires off the back of the box linked it to the antenna, and others disappeared downward. There were no switches nor dials on the box. Rico thought it was a device that added power to what he perceived to be a transmitting antenna of high frequency. He had seen enough.

He went back down slowly and quietly, relocking both doors he'd had to pick. As he finished locking the door through which he'd entered the building and was putting his lock-pick set away, he heard it. What sounded like a slight creak came from the dark shadows farther to the rear of the property, near a pile of rubble there. Some trees near the rubble cast deep shadows on the area. Rico saw something move in the shadows. Whatever it was had red eyes.

Rico decided to approach it. "Hell," he said to himself, "I've got lots of firepower on my belt. Whoever or whatever it is ain't really no threat to me. It hasn't shot at me so far. Let's go see what gives."

He slowly approached the thing in the shadows. What might have been a head turned to watch him as he came nearer, the two red 'eyes' glowing bright. Suddenly the thing said in clear English, in a human-sounding voice, "I want you to come with me now!"

In the dark shadows of the moonless night Rico was unable to discern what exactly it was that was talking to him. It reached for him but Rico backed away. He noticed the hand that reached for him had only three fingers and an opposing thumb. The fingers looked metallic.

"Keep your moldy mitts offa me!"

"You must come with me now. That is an orderrr." The *r*'s trilled in a non-human way. That was enough to set Rico walking and then running away from the thing. It came stumping after him, followed him out of the deep shadows near the abandoned store and out into the dimly lit street. A lone lamp burned on a pole a quarter mile away, offering poor illumination to the scene. The thing came faster and faster. Rico ran for his life.

Rico ducked into an alley, thinking he could hide from the thing, but the creature stopped at the alleyway, turned to and fro, seemed to sniff the air, and came down the alley after him. Rico ran again.

As he raced along, Rico wondered if it was being controlled by someone using the red eyes for feedback or if it was programmed to do certain things. Rico suspected it was put on the store premises by Farchex the robot-maker to scare away anyone – like the boy who lost the finger – who tried to see what was going on inside the old abandoned store.

Rico felt like his attempt to escape the thing had started close to ten minutes ago, but it might have been only a minute, probably less. No matter where he went he could hear it following, its tread not unlike the *ka-chung, ka-chung* of the Cybermen on Doctor Who, but much quieter and a lot faster.

The usual residents of the desert town who sat out at night to avoid the heat and horrors of their mud homes were all gone. They'd given up on the night, largely because it was close to three o'clock in the morning. No one but Rico and the thing were moving in the back streets of Timbuktu.

Rico had been heading south in the direction of his hotel, but then decided to lead the critter to the outskirts of town to the east, which was lots closer than the hotel. He dodged from street to street, barely keeping ahead of the thing. Rico was quite sure it was a robot but there was a bare chance it was someone dressed up to scare him, scare anyone who got near that old abandoned store. If it was a disguise it was a really good one.

"It moves like a human," he told himself, "but I'm sure it's a frickin' robot! One of Farchex' animated tricks comin' to get me. Damned thing finds me no matter where I hide." Rico huffed and puffed along yet another dark street, pausing only long enough to look behind him to see if 'it' was still there. It was.

As he raced along one of the streets heading east he tripped and fell. The thing kept coming. Rico rolled onto his back and shouted, "Stop!", but all it did was come faster with its eyes glowing brighter. Rico had his Daly Hi-Power out and, from the old Elmer Keith back-rested position, gun held steady against his raised right knee, he took a shot at one of the red eyes of the oncoming horror.

The crash of the shot ripped through the still of the desert night. He soon heard the sounds and voices of people moving in their houses, aroused by the noisy intrusion, so foreign to the town. Were they waking, they may have wondered, from good dreams into a nightmare of more terrorist activity, like what hit Timbuktu a few years ago? A small herd of goats a quarter mile away gave vent to the pitiful vocalizations of their sudden fright.

The robot stopped on the impact of the bullet with its red 'eye.' Its head began spinning, slowly circling around and around, then spinning faster until it was nearly a blur. Despite its now-useless head, the thing took a few steps in Rico's direction, then staggered like a drunk and fell to the ground with a resounding crash. Its legs began thrashing as though it were still running after the man, raising a cloud of dust where it lay.

Rico got up, ducked down the next cross street, and found a dark place to stop. Before he got out of sight of the robot he looked to make sure it was down for good. It was.

Keeping to the shadows and generally heading south, Rico cautiously made his way back to his hotel. Here and there lights came on in some of the dwellings, but he avoided them all. It took him a while to find the hotel, and the sun was starting to enlighten the world of Timbuktu when he finally made his way up to his room.

He lay on his bed, stared at the ceiling, and thought long and hard about everything he had seen that night. Finally sleep overcame him.

CHAPTER 21
Taking Action

Rico was roused late in the morning by the two girls beating on his door. He was too sleepy to move, so they unlocked his door and came in to find him still in bed, weary and groggy from the night's efforts. They ordered coffee and when it came, Roxy began pouring it into him. Mary opened the curtains and the window, and they both sat on the bed waiting for answers to their many questions about his night's adventures.

"Did you find him? When did you get back here?" Mary asked.

"I thought I heard a shot, but was basically asleep. Did you have any trouble?" Roxy asked. "Any wounds?"

"Gabbababba podunk. Whaflappa? Okay. Er, um. Found the place. Saw no one in there. Broke in, the back way. Heard a hum from the basement. Locked door with no picking hole to the basement. Dunno if someone was down there. There's a booster amplifier on the roof for the antenna. Nothing at all within the confines of the above-ground parts of the old building but some trash. However...." Rico swigged a slug of coffee. "What? No rolls?"

"No. Keep going!" Roxy filled his coffee cup. She kept her roll hidden behind her back.

Mary said, "You want a roll in bed with honey?"

"No! Not now! Too tired. Hey! You've got a roll!" He glared at Roxy.

"No I don't." Roxy dropped the roll behind her back onto a piece of paper towel she'd put there. She showed her hidden hand to Rico.

"Where was I? Oh, and then there was the robot."

"What?!" Mary and Roxy said together. "Tell us!"

"Not until you get me a roll!"

That service was quickly provided from a tray of them Roxy had hidden under the bed before Rico was fully awake. Roll in hand, Rico told of his adventures with the red-eyed monster, which he slew deftly (he said) with one shot from his trusty *pistola*.

"So, my girlfriends, what do we do now?"

Roxy said, "I think it's time we went and got him. Our pilot's still waiting at the airport hotel. Unless he gave up on us and flew home."

"Jeez," said Rico, "I forgot about him. So, do we just go and bang on the door? If we go inside to the locked door that won't open, and beat on that, Farchex can stay downstairs forever and we lose."

"How about a crowbar?" asked Mary. "Would that get us in?"

"Might. The door," Rico replied, "looked like heavy wood. Not metal. Unless it's booby trapped. Got any C4?"

"No," replied Roxy. "The U.N. guys probably do. How about some sort of battering ram? Were there any raw materials there to make one?"

"No. There was a bunch of dirt, some old blocks from another dead building, but I don't recall seeing any timbers nor rocks that we could use to ram the door. Here's the thing. The door to his basement might be booby trapped. So we want to open it from a distance if that's possible."

Mary spoke up. "Guys, I saw cans of Goex black powder at one of the variety stores we looked into the other day. If we can get one or two of those we could make a fuse, rig it to the can of powder and try to blow the door."

"That would do," said Rico. He shrugged into his shirt and shoes. He'd never bothered to remove his trousers when he got back to the room. "I say we go there, knock on the door, try to force it gently so we don't trip a booby trap, and if that don't work we blow it."

"Let's go!" Roxy got up and headed for the door. Out they all went.

They ate, got the necessary supplies, verified the continuing presence of Farchex with the CIA gadget, and made sure the pilot was still available to take them home. Rico made some lengthy long-distance phone calls, which took up more of the day. By mutual consent they decided to wait until nearly nightfall for their assault. By the time they got to the old store building the shadows were already black and impenetrable, though the sky overhead still showed good light. A dry breeze blew in off the desert and the trees around the building gently quivered. They knocked on the front door and, as expected, got no response. Treading carefully, they made their way to the back door. Again they knocked. Rico tried the door, which was still locked. He quickly picked the lock and cautiously swung the door open. Nothing was there that hadn't been there before, so the trio entered. Roxy peered into the front room and then they all went to the door to the basement.

"Now this door might be triggering a bomb, or it might release nasty gas, anything to give us fits." Rico tried the handle and found it to be open. "Whoa! This is not good," he said. "It might be a trap. It might mean no one's in – but I still hear that slight hum from under the floor."

Roxy said, "Let's see what's behind the door first. Open it, Rico."

"Yeah," he replied. "Like in that movie about the search for the holy grail. The guy says, 'Asps! Very dangerous! You go first!' " He found a long stick and slowly pushed opened the door, which swung heavily inward. Nothing happened. He approached it and inspected everything around the edge and on the jamb. He saw nothing.

"What are those holes?" asked Mary, indicating the edge of the door.

Roxy said, "They look like receptacles for a series of bars, like on a vault door. But the door is wood, is it not? Rico?"

"Yes, it does seem to be wood, but it's heavy."

They could not yet see the edges of the door to inspect it.

"No snakes, so that's good." Rico looked upward. There was a light inside the door that was on, and there were no obvious booby traps. "Guys, does this seem like a trap to you?"

"Yes," said Roxy.

"So, what do we do?" asked Mary.

"Why'nt you both stay here and let me go see what's in there," said Rico.

"No!" exclaimed Roxy. "In for a penny...."

"Okay," replied Rico. "But if we all get pounded, don't blame me."

The three passed through the basement door onto a landing, from which steps led downward along a well-lighted corridor. They examined the edge of the door as they went through it.

The outer handle, they noted, was a simple latch with a corresponding inner handle. The inside of the door had a second, centrally located handle. When Rico twisted the second inner handle several steel bars extended outward all around the door. With the door shut the steel bars would extend into the holes in the door jamb, locking the door much like a vault. Rico commented, "This looks like my gun-vault door, except that it's set in wood, not steel."

Down the steps they went, always looking for trip wires, microswitches, light sources that when broken by someone walking through the beam could trigger...anything. The stairs had been leading them downward to the west, toward the front of the building. Halfway down the stairs, perhaps eight feet below the floor level, was a landing, and then the stairs continued back the other direction, leading down another six or eight feet underground to the east. At the bottom of the stairs was another landing with an open doorway to the right. As Rico in the lead carefully and slowly peered around the corner he suddenly understood why Farchex wanted to escape to Timbuktu.

The open doorway led to a huge room, well lighted by a series of lamps placed around the walls, the room being at least as large as the old store above them. The room was filled with treasures of all sorts. Small marble figurines were in glass cases. Wall hangings were rich Persian carpets. Rows of shelves held hand-carved ivory items, each a work of art. Oil paintings were on the wall, too. One was a Reubens, another a Van Gogh. A dozen more paintings were obviously fine art, some from obscure painters, each worth a fortune. The floor was covered in tiles, with colored decorations inlaid in it. There were no rugs on the floor. There was a small table, a desk with its roll-front closed, several chairs, some padded. There was a couch along one wall. Four gold- and jewel-encrusted swords hung on another wall. A standing cabinet held ancient firelocks, matchlocks and early wheellocks, each with heavy gold inlay and engraving, one with an ivory stock. Pots and bowls with ancient designs were under glass. Other cases held gold and silver plates, cups, even eating utensils. Gold decorative castings were in other cases. All the things were treasures from ancient Timbuktu, some dating back five hundred years or more. It was like walking into a museum room, but it was far more crowded than any museum display room.

No one said anything. No one else was in the room.

A slight hum pervaded the space.

Two doors led off the room, one off the east wall, toward the nearest edge of town and the desert beyond, and the other in the south wall.

The east door led to yet another room filled with riches. A darkened corridor on the far side of the room led slightly downward and farther eastward, but Rico decided to take a look behind the second door in the main room first. It was full of electronic equipment. Against the far wall was the source of the hum, a big fan sucking clean air into the room from above somewhere. There was enough evidence in the room to show that the red-eyed robot Rico had shot had originated there. A second robot seemed to be under construction on one of the tables. The monitor screens and radio-like equipment in the room were enough to indicate there was at least the possibility of some human control and observation of Rico's red-eyed robot from that basement room.

"Let's take a look down this corridor past the second room of goodies, eh? Are you two with me?"

Mary said, "I'll just stay here and fill my pockets with these goodies, if you don't mind. I see an ivory carving I simply *must* have!" She wandered away from the other two, down a row of glass-covered showcases.

"Nuts!" exclaimed Roxy. "Let's follow Rico and watch him get his head blown off. Won't that be fun?"

"Hey! That's my head you're blowing off. Watch it!"

"So...you want me to not blow you off?" Roxy smiled.

"Damn! Not here! Mary's watching."

"What are you two talking about now?" Mary asked as she pulled herself away from eyeballing the fine art in the room and joined the other two.

"Nothing. Rico's making passes at me." Roxy smirked.

"Come on," said Rico. "Let's see how far out into the desert this path leads us."

They had not got twenty feet down the eastward corridor, sloping into the ground, when they heard the first explosion. The sound came from in front of them, and then a second smaller explosion came from behind them. The roof of the corridor began to give way up ahead of them.

"Run! Run for the entrance!" Rico spun around and urged his two friends in front of them. The athletic women quickly left Rico in their dust, but he wasn't far behind. Through the second treasure room and into the first they hared, and then up the stairs as fast as they could go. The door was closed, it looked slightly bulged, and the handle was blown off. The locking bolts around the edge of the door were all driven into the locking recesses in the edge of the door opening by the force of the second explosion. The door was thoroughly locked tight. They were trapped!

CHAPTER 22
Blowing It

Roxy was at the door first, and gave it a quick inspection. She dug her fingers into the hole in the door where the handle had been located, to no avail. "Shit! The bolts are locked into the wall. Blown into the wall. So what do we do now?"

Rico said, "Lemme look back the way we came. There might be light at the end of the tunnel." He went back to the corridor off the second treasure room and peered down it, but it was choked off with fallen dirt, rocks and lots of sand. He came back and said, "No go. This way or nothing."

Roxy repeated, "So what do we do now?"

Mary replied, "We could wait. Or...."

"Wait my ass," said Roxy. "I've got a hair appointment in the morning – in New York City. We've gotta get out."

Rico agreed. "Yes, we've gotta get outa here. He might release gas, or herds of snakes, and no one in the world knows we're stuck down here. Roxy's hair looks like hell, so that appointment is critical. So how can we get out?"

Mary again, "There are swords downstairs. Or...."

"Nuts!" Roxy ran her fingers through her hair.

Mary said, "We could make a battering ram out of some of the heavy gold objects downstairs. Or...."

Roxy said, "We could use Rico's head for a battering ram." Finally she got the message. "Mary! Or what??"

"Or we could use these cans of black powder that we bought on the way here and blow the shit out of the door."

Rico said, "Mary, I think this is the beginning of a beautiful friendship!"

With care they placed two one-pound cans of Goex FFFg powder carefully on the door where they though it would do the most good. They got some heavy blocks that were part of the decoration in the treasure room and stuck them against the powder cans to increase the force of the explosion toward the door. They considered blowing the wall next to the door, but the wall was thick mud bricks and the door was at least partly wood, so the door it was. They took the caps off the cans to expose the powder inside to the flame from whichever can blew first. Using the powder from another can they jury-rigged a fuse with a piece of thin cloth Roxy found in the treasure room. They ran some more powder to the fuse to give them time to escape downstairs. Rico insisted on being the match man. The two girls went all the way down to the bottom of the stairs to the far side of the treasure room and got behind the couch. Mary hollered, "All set, Rico!"

"Here we go, ladies!" Rico lit the fast-burning fuse and barely made it to the bend in the staircase before the blast went off. The heart of the door disintegrated, leaving a few scraps of steel where the locking bolts were mounted and a fringe of wood on the edges. The three friends stepped through the ragged new doorway into the old building with ease. By that time it was full dark outside and they didn't want to stick around to see who might come to inspect the source of the blast. They disappeared into the shadows of the night and made their way quickly back to their hotel.

Over drinks they talked about the situation. Rico's ears were still ringing from the blast. "Damn!" said Rico, shaking his head to try to clear his ears. "Our quarry got away. He expected to trap us in there, go away for some months or so, and then come back to his treasures, clean out the bodies, and get on with his life."

"We could go to his airplane," suggested Mary. "Maybe get the local cops to impound it."

Roxy asked, "Is there a chance Farchex got trapped by the explosions? Do we know he was even in there when the first two blasts went off? We checked him early today with our tracker. Maybe he left his cell phone down there as a decoy, and he's been gone a while. I mean, the guy's into robotics. He knows his stuff. So he could have arranged this trap beforehand, you know, set it all up and when we started down that corridor we somehow set off a signal to blow the whole thing."

"Crap," replied Rico. "You're right." He picked up the phone and called their pilot, Apeez Uvrok, diligently waiting in the airport hotel for them to come along with their prisoner. "Apeez, sorry to disturb you so late. Did you notice a twin Baron leaving the airport recently?"

"Yes, Mr. Rico, it left here this afternoon. And no, you did not disturb me."

"Okay, we'll be along in the morning to fly back to Casablanca. See you then." Rico carefully placed the room phone handset on the cradle, walked to the window and peered into the darkness. Then he began to curse softly. This went on for a while. When he was done he turned back to the two women, sat down, and poured himself another drink from the Scotch bottle, hefty and straight. "Simply blunderful."

"He could be anywhere in the world now." Roxy got up and paced the room.

Mary seemed unperturbed. "He can go anywhere, but where's the most likely place for him to go? Back to the U.S. to see his so-called partner. Maybe not immediately, but eventually. He can't go back to Casablanca, at least not right away, because he knows we know about it, and he'll believe we told the local cops about him. We'll check with his company when we get back there. But Rico, don't you have to get back to the 'States? We sure do."

"Actually, yes. Your reasoning is excellent. He'll have to show up in Atlanta at some point, if only to take some revenge on Luftin for letting us come here."

Roxy was unhappy. "Piss! We failed. Why did we fail? We should have locked up that airplane. Put one of us on guard there if nothing better. But no, we didn't. And now our quarry is gone to the four corners of the earth. There's no guarantee he'll go to Atlanta. He could sit in Paris for several years, let his company run itself. He could phone in instructions and orders to make sure it stays running. It's all your fault, Rico Morgan."

That night the trio had a last dinner together at Rick's Cafe with plenty of wine, then went back to their hotel rooms and got rip-roaring drunk on the remains of the Scotch and gin and wine that was left there. The next morning they met with Apeez and flew back to Casablanca, checked the Farchex factory to make sure the owner had not shown up, checked with the airport to see if his plane had returned (it hadn't), and then made their reservations to fly back to the 'States.

The girls were going to DC and Rico to Atlanta, but they were able to fly together. On the ground in DC Rico bid the girls goodbye with promises all around to stay in touch, and then he caught a flight from DC to Atlanta.

CHAPTER 23
Atlanta Revisited

Rico Morgan was on his own again. The two ladies who helped him in his adventures in Casablanca and Timbuktu were far away in DC telling their sad tale to their boss at CIA, telling him that they failed to collect the man they went after. They'd probably get a slap on the wrist, Rico thought, and get sent to their rooms. Their agency really doesn't give a crap whether they caught him or not, Rico reasoned. They have the Aussies to persecute Farchex, so why should CIA bother with the guy any more, now that they know what he did and why.

Rico was back at the hotel room he rented the first time he went to Atlanta. The only friendly face Rico knew in that town was Manny Arkald, who ran his gym in Atlanta. The last time Rico saw him Manny expressed a desire to help Rico in some sort – any sort – of criminal investigation if he ever needed Manny's help. This just might be that time, thought Rico. He phoned Manny.

"Manny, I need your help. I can't do what I need to do alone. I need to entrap a guy...catch him, I mean. An important guy who's been committing fraud on his own company and might be involved in murder. I might find him with a dead man's wife, maybe aboard a boat, but most likely over at the woman's house. More important, I need to see if he meets with another guy coming in from Casablanca. The Casablanca guy is in partnership with the Atlanta guy to defraud the Atlanta guy's own company, which doesn't make any sense unless you know the details. The Casablanca guy got away from us in Africa and I think he's headed here to Atlanta. Also, one or both of these men are guilty of murder. This can be one dangerous operation, or series of operations, my friend. Are you still interested?"

"Hell, Rico, I told you I'm bored shitless with the running of this gym. I mean, what joy can I find in a bunch of fat-ass people coming in here to get all sweaty, and then I never see most of 'em again. You're damned right I'm interested. Even if I get shot at. I was in the service, ya know, got shot at back then. So yes, count me in for whatever I can do for you, or with you."

"Manny, that's great. It might get a whole lot boring before it gets interesting. I can't guarantee you'll be shot at, but I can provide that service if you really need it."

"As long as you miss, I'm in! So when do we start? What's the plan?"

"Manny, I'll see you tomorrow morning. Buy you breakfast and we can discuss it then. You pick the place and tell me where to find you."

"You got it, Mr. Detective!"

"The first thing I want to do is run surveillance on this dude, name of Luftin." Rico showed Manny a photo of Boris Luftin as they sat eating eggs at a diner near Manny's gym the next morning. "I already told you what he's been up to. I suspect the guy from Casablanca – Augie Farchex – will show up here and meet with Luftin in the next few days. It might be longer, but I think Farchex is eager to meet with his secret partner Luftin."

"Why?"

"The Casablanca guy knows we're on to him and his crooked operation. The Atlanta guy might not know all the details. What it amounts to is that Atlanta guy hired me to find out what was wrong with his computers, and I found out the Casablanca guy is sticking bad chips into Atlanta guy's computers, and Atlanta guy actually *wants* that to happen. He's trying to bankrupt his own company. If that happens he gets very rich, and can then go to Casablanca and be in business with the guy over there, who runs the same kind of company. Do you follow all that? It's kind of confusing."

"Yeah, I get it, I think. This guy here wants to bust his own company because he probably has some insurance that pays him big-time if it goes belly up. The guy in north Africa is helping him do it. But what does this guy, the north-Africa or Casablanca guy, get out of it?"

"Ultimately, money. His company, called Fortune Industries, is the main competitor to the Atlanta company, which is Luftin-Borlew, or L-B. If L-B dies, then Fortune Industries can pick up most of the business that L-B will have lost because of the phony computer problems. The pisser is, Luftin hired me to find out what's going on, and I guess he never thought I'd be able to find out. I did, and because he doesn't yet know all the details of what happened in Africa – I mean he doesn't know how much I know – I expect the Africa-based guy to show up here and fill him in."

"Got it. But why was that other guy killed? Did he know too much?"

"I suspected Herbert Harumfer was whacked because he was about to hire me to try and find out what's going on with his company's faulty computer chips. But now, knowing what I've found out about the scam, I think Herbie also might have found out something about the scam, and was killed to keep him quiet about it. He was CEO of L-B and on the board of directors of the company. If he went to the board with info like I've just told you, it'd be all over for Boris Luftin. They'd kick him out and he'd be up the creek with zero money and zero leverage. Incidentally, Luftin is having an affair with Ginny Harumfer, the wife of the dead guy."

"More motive for murder!"

"Possibly. Now, it's not entirely necessary we find Luftin banging the dead man's wife. I'm sure it happens, but can't prove anything. As I said, that affair is not really important in that it probably has nothing to do with murder nor fraud. But it's necessary to keep an eye on her because of her involvement, and because we never know who's going to show up at her house."

"What's her name? Ginny?

"The woman's name is Virginia Harumfer. Ginny. Her husband was the guy murdered by poison gas coming off his laptop some weeks ago. I want you to watch her house today. As I said, it might help lead us to the guy we can immediately arrest, this August X. Farchex, who tried to kill us in Timbuktu a few days ago. This is what he looks like." Rico gave Manny a photo of Farchex.

"In short," continued Rico, "we need whatever info we can get on these three people, Luftin, Farchex, and Ginny Harumfer. The only other one we might encounter is Becky Luftin, Boris's wife, who doesn't know and probably doesn't care what her husband is up to."

"So how are we gonna do all this?"

"The most boring thing in the world. We drive to the woman's house, sit in the car, and watch to see who comes and goes. We go to Ginny's house during the day and one of us goes to Luftin's house in the evening, so we can keep an eye out for all sorts of stuff."

"A stakeout, okay. But is there no better way to shake things up? Such as confront 'em?"

"I'm gonna confront Luftin today to see what he says. He ought not to know I've been to Timbuktu. I didn't tell him, but I'm sure he knows because I'm sure Farchex told him. So if he makes any mention of that town, that'll confirm he's talked with Farchex. Meantime, you can keep an eye on the house of one Ginny Harumfer. Here's her address. Just park where you can keep an eye on the place, say fifty yards away, and see who goes in and comes out."

"You got a picture of her?"

"No, but she lives alone at that house. Tall, dark hair, very white face."

"So you're going to see the one guy today?"

"Yep. What I'd like to do is plant a bug in Luftin's office, and I'll try to do that. I can put a tap his phone, and that's already under way." Rico didn't mention his man Yeats, at Boise Control, was already monitoring all the calls in and out of Luftin's office.

The two men left and went their separate ways, Manny to the house of Ginny Harumfer and Rico to the offices of Luftin-Borlew.

Rico gave his card to the receptionist at L-B and asked to see Boris Luftin. He was shown in immediately.

"Mr. Morgan," said Boris Luftin, shaking hands with Rico. "What news do you bring me about my computer problems? Have you solved everything?"

"Actually I've solved some of it, but not yet all of it. Your faulty chips are indeed coming from your partner August X. Farchex. He has his company load the bad ones along with good ones randomly into your motherboards, and when they arrive here, your company loads them unsuspectingly into your robotics. After so many cycles the main chip is programmed to do something random instead of what you want it to do. This disrupts the cycle and creates havoc with the machinery, which in turn creates havoc with your company. We've determined this from an analysis of proven faulty chips taken from several of the companies that have been hit with the so-called virus."

Throughout all this Boris Luftin's expression didn't change, most specifically, Rico noticed, when he called Farchex his partner.

"I see. So the only solution, I suppose, is to find a different supplier. Is there any way the companies to which I've sold equipment can test for faulty chips?"

"Yes, though it's a bit labor intensive. They can do an inspection of each of the computers, pull the heat sink off the main board and examine the central processing chip underneath the sink. If it has no name, it will have to be replaced. I have no idea how you can organize that, but that's about your only option. If you don't do that your company will continue to go down the drain, and it'll do so quickly because as more time goes by, more of the faulty chips are approaching the required number of cycles to go haywire. I presume you don't want your company to go down the drain." Rico watched Luftin closely when he said this.

Luftin blinked a few times, then said, "No, certainly not. I don't know what I'd do if this company goes bust."

"I suppose," said Rico, "you could go join the outfit making the bad chips. I understand they are also making and selling robotics machinery. Essentially, as you told me, Farchex is your main competitor. But then, that might not go down well with your shareholders."

Luftin got a bit red, turned his chair to look out the window, and breathed deeply a time or two. He then replied, "I suppose I could jump out the window. I'd like to get back at the bastard that is giving me the bad chips. Do you know why? Did you see if there's a link to my college days with the man who runs that company? Why is he trying to ruin me?"

"Why don't you ask him?" While Luftin was staring out the window Rico slipped the bug under the edge of his desk. "I suspect he's on his way to the 'States to pay you a visit. He got away from me in Timbuktu, where he fled after I paid him a social call and, essentially, called him out with the proof that he was making bad chips."

Rico intentionally left the two CIA agents out of the equation.

"Now, why in hell would he want to visit me?"

"I'm not sure he does, but he's not in Casablanca, and he bombed his place in Timbuktu...."

At this Luftin's eyes shot wide open, he gasped, and nearly jumped out of his seat. "Bombed it? I mean, er, what did he do that for? Is it completely destroyed?"

Rico wanted to say, "Relax, asshole, your share of the goodies down under the city are only blocked off a bit, and we blew a hole in the upper door to get out, and of course the UN probably has everything in there confiscated by now, so you're just as screwed as if your buddy buried it all." Instead he said, "I don't really know. I just heard about it while I was there looking for him, and I heard that from the UN guys." This was a lie, but Rico threw it out to worry Luftin. Rico also knew the UN or the town cops would surely have gone to look at what caused the blast that opened the basement door for Rico and the girls' escape. He continued his tale. "Farchex escaped in his airplane and is currently on the run, so I thought there was no more need to stay there. Basically I'm done with that part of the job for which you hired me. The murder still needs to be solved."

"Well, that's interesting." Luftin sat back in his chair and stared at the ceiling. His hand shook visibly. Finally he asked, "What's your next move, Mr. Morgan?"

"I'm going to pursue some fresh leads into the murder of your partner. How's his wife doing, by the way?"

"Ginny's fine, er, I mean I've heard that Virginia is doing well enough. Now, Mr. Morgan, you'll have to excuse me. I've got a, er, business meeting in a few minutes. Please send me an invoice for your expenses so far." He stood up, hand still trembling, and a touch of sweat on his upper lip. Rico was getting close to the heart of the matter and Luftin didn't like it at all. He extended his hand to Rico and said, "Please let me know if you find anything out about Herbert's murder. And thank you for coming."

Rico twisted the knife a bit more. "Good luck with your clients, arranging for them to exchange the faulty chips." Rico knew Luftin had exactly no intention of doing anything about that little problem. He touched Luftin's limp paw and left the room.

Outside in his rental car he called Yeats. "Are you getting it, my friend?"

Yeats, the head of Rico's Boise Control operation in Idaho, replied in his thick Indian accent, "Loud and clear, kind sir. That is an excellent bug."

"It oughta be. Darned thing cost me over two hundred bucks."

"I will keep you posted, kind sir, as to what I hear. I will also send you a computer link to my readout so you can keep up with all the conversations that come from within that office. Whenever there is voice activity my recorder gathers it in, and you can read it for your own self when you have the time. But of course if I hear anything urgent I will let you know immediately to your cell phone. You...*do* have it with you, kind sir?"

Yeats well knew Rico hated cell phones.

"Yes, of course, Yeats, always with me, and of course you know I'm on it right now."

"Yes, indeedy, kind sir. I presume you are on your way to watch his house?"

"Not right away," replied Rico. "I've gotta see the Atlanta cop to let him know what's going on, and see if he has any new information. Then I'll check with Manny to see what he's seen, watching the woman's house. Too bad we don't have more bugs in the houses, eh?"

"That is correct, Mr. Rico, but I think you have the bug in the very best place to find our quarry."

"Thanks, my friend." Rico broke the connection.

Rico drove to the police station and asked to see Inspector Ralf Raktum. Ralf brought Rico to his inner sanctum and, over lots of coffee, Rico told Ralf of his adventures in Casablanca and Timbuktu. He ended the long story by saying, "So I think he, Farchex, might be on his way to pay a visit to his partner Luftin. We're watching Luftin's house and that of his lady friend, Ginny Harumfer."

"That's quite a tale, Mr. Morgan. So you think Luftin's trying to destroy his own company? Let me add to the mysteries. We talked to Herbert Harumfer's lawyer and found evidence that Herbie was about to file for divorce. His lawyer had prepared the papers, but nothing was yet signed. Mrs. Harumfer, Ginny, was about to become single. The lawyer said there was no new will, but that Herbie had indicated he wanted to change it, as well as get the divorce. That might have given her a motive – if she had known about it. But of course her husband was killed by a message sent to his computer. How Virginia Harumfer could have done that is shady, at best."

"That's a key point, Inspector Raktum."

"Call me Ralf. What's a key point?"

"The key point seems to be, did she know about the upcoming divorce? If she did, then did she know about the killer laptops? And if so, how did she know?"

"Do you plan to pay her another visit? You could maybe ask her if she knew about the divorce. I have no reason to see her, and my being a cop might scare her into all kinds of denial."

"I might have to do that. I'll keep you posted."

Rico phoned Manny, who had nothing. "Rico, I've watched that place like a hawk lookin' for a mouse, and no one's gone in nor out. It'll be dark soon and if there ain't no lights come on, that means there's no one in there. Should I stay on target?"

"Hate to say it, but yes, that's the plan. I'm going to drive to Luftin's house but I'll come by where you are and drop off a burger, if that's okay."

"What do I do if I gotta pee? Like now?"

"I'll hurry and bring an extra large drink cup. You can use it and then discretely dump it out your door when it gets dark."

"Okay. Hurry!"

Rico watched the Luftin household that evening until nearly midnight. All he saw was that Luftin's wife Becky came home around eight, clearly dressed for golf. Rico guessed she had probably eaten with friends at the club house. Boris Luftin came home about nine, having apparently eaten out. The house lights went off a bit after eleven, and Rico sat in the car diligently for another hour.

At midnight Rico phoned Manny again. "Anything?"

"Yes. No one was here most of the day, but the lady of the house came home a little after nine tonight, all alone. She was wearing a dress. Looked like she could've met someone for dinner. You?"

"My man got to his house around nine, so maybe they had dinner together. The lady of the house, Becky, came in earlier. Let's call it a day."

The next day bright and early Rico sat in the car with Manny, watching the Harumfer house. Ginny worked in the front yard a bit on the flowers, then disappeared. By noon no one had come. Rico was about to leave Manny to his boredom when a car came roaring down the street. It braked hard and drove into Ginny's driveway. When the driver got out, Rico said, "That's him! That's August Farchex, the bastard who tried to kill us in Timbuktu. What in hell is he doing here with Ginny Harumfer?"

"Let's wait and see," said Manny. "You gotta be patient, Rico. Didn't you tell me that yesterday?"

Rico mumbled something under his breath, and the two sat and waited.

An hour later out came August with Ginny right behind him. He turned and kissed her, got in his car and drove serenely away.

CHAPTER 24
Bye Bye Ginny

"Sonofabitch!" That was all Rico could say as he and Manny watched Farchex drive away from Ginny Harumfer's house.

"So they are lovers, it would seem." Manny shook his head. "Rico, I'm confused. I thought this woman was having an affair with the head of Luftin Industries. Did I get it wrong?"

"No, Manny, you got it right. But this is a switcheroo. Ginny and August are now a pair. She's either banging them both or scheming...in some mighty deep way. How could he have managed to get this going from Casablanca? They look like they're comfortable friends here, not just casual lovers. It's like they've done this before a whole lot. She must've flown over there, or he flew here, a whole lot over the past...what, year or more?"

"Does this change everything?"

"I dunno. I gotta talk with Yeats." Rico took out his cell phone which had been turned off, and found three unanswered messages from Yeats. He immediately called Yeats and asked, "What's up?"

"O dearie me! Mister Morgan it would be good if you left your cell phone turned on so I can give you important information."

Rico apologized profusely. "Yeats, I promise I'll have it on day and night. So, what's up?"

"August Farchex was in the office of Boris Luftin this morning. The conversation was about murder, lies, plans for the future, and a whole lot of other things. The most important little piece of the lengthy conversation is this...listen carefully." Yeats played a short bit of the recorded conversation to Rico:

> "Dammit, Boris, you never should have told Ginny about the killer laptop. If Herb was still alive we'd be home free."
>
> "I never told her anything! She must have overheard me on the phone to you, something like that. Once she knew about it she probably looked in my files to find the fuckin' code, and that was it."
>
> "So now we're up for murder on account of her! Just ducky, buddy."

Rico looked at Manny and said to Yeats, "Kind sir, I will never have my cell phone off again. That's the best sort of information. It proves they're together in this, and establishes excellent proof that Ginny Harumfer is the murderer, not one of those guys. But Yeats, I have something for you, my friend. We just saw Mr. Farchex leave the Harumfer household, and when he left, he kissed Ginny goodbye."

"That is not good. That means something very dirty is afoot. I will look into that aspect."

"Yeats, see if you can find evidence of him or her flying back and forth to Casablanca over the past year."

"Mister Morgan, I am already doing that. Thank you for telling me my job." Yeats cut the connection.

Rico left Manny at the house of the Harumfer woman and returned in his rental car to his hotel, where he listened to the full recording of the conversation between Farchex and Luftin. There was a greeting between the colluding frauds, and then it quickly got into the serious matters in which Rico had the most interest.

[*Farchex:*] "So Morgan came here. I knew he got out of my trap down in the vault. Did he tell you anything about it?"

"What? You had him locked in the vault?"

"Yeah, him and whoever was with him. I knew he was going to come back because he destroyed my harum-scarum robot the previous night. I was watching him through its eyes and the bastard shot it. Then the damned police showed up when someone called 'em about the thing kicking up dust in the street. They called the UN guys, and they took control of it. Busted it all up trying to shut it off. So I knew Morgan was gonna come back. I thought I'd got away from him and his bitches in Casablanca, but they traced me to Timbuktu and showed up a few days after I got there."

[*Luftin:*] "Who were these bitches?"

"One, maybe both, were CIA."

"Oh shit!"

"Anyway, I set a trap for whoever went into the vault. I locked the outer doors to the old store so the kids wouldn't get in there. I knew Morgan picked the lock the night before, so he could get in easy. The trap was set to keep him underground forever. There was no way to get out. I made sure the back entrance and the path leading to it was blasted shut when they tripped a light signal, and I had it blow the door charge too, which locked the bars into the door jamb. He should've been locked underground there for years. But no, he gets out and shows up here. Piss!"

[*Luftin;*] "He said something about the place being bombed. I was worried our stash of valuables might have been hurt."

"Not by my blasts. I'm too careful for that. I know that door was locked like a damned vault. But he got past it!"

"How did he prove your chips were the bad ones?"

"Fucker went to Portugal, broke in to the factory there at night and stole some of the bad chips. Got past my snake, too. Then he comes to my office at Casablanca and confronts me. I had my girl Sum Ting hold him there while I drove to the airport and flew south."

"Well, he's here and he's after us. After you, actually. He has not let on he knows anything nasty about me."

"Might be a good idea to get rid of him once and for all."

"Maybe. But what about the women? The CIA agents? I had no idea Morgan would figure out all this stuff. Now the CIA knows too. So is it worthwhile screwing with him?"

[*Farchex:*]"Where is he now?"

"Says he's checking out some new info on the murder."

Here followed the conversation that Yeats already played for Rico, the two conspirators belaboring each other about the needless death of Herbert Harumfer, caused by his wife. What came after was also of great interest to the private eye:

"Remember, Augie, we have not yet committed murder."

"Nuts, Boris, we're accessories to murder because we set up the damned killer laptops. We're goin' down for that if we ever get caught."

"Maybe the best idea is to just get outa the U.S. Heck, I could live happily in Casablanca for the rest of my life."

"Yeah. Well, Boris, I've got an appointment across town. See you later."

August Farchex left the office then, presumably on his way to keep his hot date with Ginny. There were sounds as though Luftin was pacing the room, mumbling to himself. Then he left the office, and that was the end of the recording.

Rico sat back and stared out the window. It was nearly time for him to leave to stake out Luftin's home when his cell phone rang.

"Mr. Morgan, this is Boris Luftin. You might want to know that August Farchex arrived, and came here to my office. He left it this morning. I've had meetings all day and this is the first chance I've had to call you."

"I see," said Rico. *So the dogs were turning on each other.* "Do you know where he is now, or where he's staying?"

"No, he didn't tell me where he is staying. Had some appointment across town, he told me. Anyway, I thought you'd like to know."

"Thank you, Mr. Luftin. I'll be in touch."

"Well," thought Rico. "Did Ginny call him? Let him know his partner is boning her? Naw, I don't think she'd tell Luftin that, much less about the visit. She and Augie seemed too happy. So now Boris is trying to get Farchex out of the picture so he can go to Casablanca and take over the factory."

Rico phoned Yeats at Boise Control. "*Amigo,* I have news. The head of Luftin-Borlew is trying to get the head of his rival company, Fortune Industries in Casablanca, jailed. Boris Luftin just phoned me and told me his 'partner' is in town. That sounds like he's trying to get rid of a rival, not help a partner."

"And why, kind sir, do you tell me this?"

"Er, well, I uh, I wanted to talk with someone. See what someone else thinks about this."

"I think you are right, sir. Mr. Luftin does indeedy want his so-called partner to get arrested. Can you arrest him if you find him?"

"I have that international warrant, but I really don't have any proof that he's done anything over here. Of course he tried to kill us in Timbuktu."

"Or it might have been a gas explosion that got you trapped in the basement there after you illegally broke into his building."

"Damn it, Yeats...!"

"I suggest you might talk with the local police, who would surely want to know of the presence of this man. By the way, we have found evidence of half a dozen flights by Virginia Harumfer to Casablanca in the past year."

Rico said, "That means she was going there while her husband was still alive."

"It would seem so, yes."

"Aargh!" Rico broke the connection. Then he paced the room. Yeats was right. The only proven things Farchex had done for which there was evidence was bribing an Australian official. That, the local police would say, was a job for the Aussie international cops. Rico had the bogus chips, which he'd sent to Yeats for examination, but again there was only Rico's word against Farchex's about what was being done with them, much less who actually made them. Rico was basically screwed. Rico's recording of Farchex and Luftin in Luftin's office was actually bordering on illegal, so that was also useless as evidence. He needed something concrete. Maybe he could go see what Ginny had to say about killing her husband by emailing a magic code to his computer.

"Nuts," he thought, "that won't fly either. She sent a message on her computer to his. There's no way to tell where that message came from in the first place, and if it's traced to her, she can claim innocence that it was deadly. So what do I do now?"

After considerable thought Rico decided to go see Ginny Farchex. For one thing, he could check to see if the photo of her and Boris Luftin was still on display in her living room.

It was late afternoon when Rico knocked on Ginny's door. She let him in, and said, "Excuse the mess, Mr. Morgan. I'm trying to get this place ready to sell. I'm going away."

"Oh? Where are you headed," asked Rico. Clear signs of packing things were in evidence. All the photos and personal items that had decorated the fireplace mantel and the fancy tables were gone, along with the fancy tables. Several large sealed boxes were in the living room.

"I'm not absolutely sure yet, but definitely overseas. Maybe Paris. I'm sick of living here with nothing to do. I kind of miss Herbert, and this place is getting on my nerves. It's kinda ghostly, if you know what I mean."

Rico did indeed know what she meant. Her guilt from killing her husband was starting to come back on her. He said, "I can sympathize with that. I lost a good friend a couple years back, name of Terry, guy I went to school with. I keep expecting him to call me. So, how soon are you leaving? You said you're going to sell this place?"

"I'll list it with a realtor after I'm out of here. I have a lawyer friend who can take care of any formalities, so I don't have to stick around for the sale. I hope to leave in a week or so. The sooner the better, as far as I'm concerned." She tossed her black hair out of her eyes. Smudges of dust marred her pale face.

Rico noted she mentioned a lawyer friend. Could that lawyer have told her that her husband was about to file for divorce? Rico probed. "Oh, that's great. A family lawyer is a handy person to have around. Helps with all kinds of problems that a couple like you and Herbert might've run into."

"Yes," Ginny replied. "He's been a part of our family ever since we were married."

So Rico knew, then, that Ginny had indeed found out about the upcoming divorce, which would have given her the incentive to send the killing message to her husband. He wondered if she and the lawyer were lovers.

"Have you heard from Boris?" Rico asked.

"Yes! The company is getting worse and worse. A review in the Wall Street Journal said that the company will be out of business in six months...maybe sooner. Boris just called to complain to me. Asked if I knew what was going on. Caught me up on the bad news."

"I suppose you're selling your stock...?"

"Oh yes! No point in sitting on a sinking ship. Which reminds me. He's selling his boat. He's gotta raise cash to help his company, I guess."

"Okay, Ginny, I'll get out of your hair. Good luck in your travels."

Rico made a beeline for the police department to the office of Inspector Ralf Raktum. "Ralf, she's running. I know she's the one who murdered her husband. She learned from her lawyer that Herbert was about to file for divorce, and I guess she wanted him to croak before he cut her off. She sent the killing message to his deadly computer."

"And how do we prove all this in a court of law? Mr. Morgan, we...."

"Call me Rico!"

"Rico, we can't do a damned thing to stop her. We have your recording that she pulled the plug – er, sent the message – that killed her husband. That recording would have close to zero credibility in court. Your recording was justified by this office, specifically by me, but a judge might not like it at all. There's no way, even if we found her fingerprints on the computer she used to send the message, that we can put her in jail for this."

"So she's gonna fly. How can we prevent that?"

"If she confesses to you or to a viable witness that she sent the message, then we have something. Otherwise, bye bye Ginny."

CHAPTER 25
August

Rico joined Manny late the afternoon of the next day, and they watched Ginny's house together. Manny filled him in on the activities. "Rico, no one's been here but a UPS truck. It came and picked up a bunch of boxes and took 'em away. What about the furniture?"

"Ginny said she was gonna list the house with most of the existing furniture, so all she has to get out is her personal crap."

"Man, Rico, we all collect a lotta crap along the way, don't we?"

"Tell me about it, *amigo*. I've got *buildings* full of stuff I haven't touched in ten years, back in Idaho."

"I know whatcha mean. You oughta see the basement of my house. A lotta my daughter's stuff is still in the basement with all my things, and even more in the attic. Yuk! When my wife died I hung onto a lot of her things for a while, but it just made me unhappy. So it went to GoodWill."

It was near sundown and Rico was unhappy. "Manny, what say we go get some dinner and talk this situation over. Might help to clarify it all."

"Shouldn't one of us keep an eye on this place?"

"Why? I just came from the cop shop yesterday and they verified we can't do anything about Ginny-the-murderer unless she's willing to sign a written confession she murdered her husband by sending a coded message to him. She could claim ignorance and no judge would touch it. So she's leaving, and we'll have to let her go."

"What if that fat guy shows up here again? Or what if both guys show up? What do they do, flip a coin to see who's going to bed Ginny tonight?"

"If they do both show up maybe they'll have a shootout and do our job for us. Come on, leave your car here and we can come back later, see what's going on."

They drove to a restaurant Manny knew, a few miles from the stakeout. The dinner was excellent, as was the wine Manny suggested along with it.

Rico and Manny returned to the stakeout after dinner, and there was a car in the Ginny's driveway, parked behind her VW. It looked like the rental they'd seen when August Farchex visited her the day before.

Not long after they settled in to watch the house another car drove into the driveway, blocking the first car. It was a fancy one. Boris Luftin got out and went into the house like he owned it.

As far away as Rico and Manny were from the house, they heard the sudden shouting. This went on for a while. Rico drove a bit closer to the house, "Just in case," as Rico said.

It was quiet for maybe ten minutes. Then they heard loud voices, glass breaking, and more loud talk. A woman's voice joined in. Unfortunately the men outside could not hear what was being said.

Rico, still in the driver's seat, said to Manny, "Stay here, but move to the driver's seat and be ready to go. I'm gonna sneak up closer and see if I can hear what's going on."

As Rico got out of the driver's seat the loud voices rose to shouts, and the two men could understand some of the words. They heard the woman, presumably Ginny, shout, "Never!"

"That's it then, you worthless bitch!" That, Rico thought, sounded like Boris.

Both Rico and Manny had just stepped out of the car as this was playing out. Rico was about to start sneaking to the house when they distinctly heard the other man say, "You'll never do it, you bastard!"

"Bet me, fucker!"

Three shots rang out. Ginny screamed, After a few seconds she yelled, "Leave him alone!"

"I need this!" yelled Boris.

Suddenly the front door flew open and Boris ran out, made a dash to his car, and in a frantic burst of energy backed to the street and drove away, wheels spinning, engine howling.

As soon as Boris came racing out of the house Rico made a beeline for the driver's seat of the rental car again, and Manny jumped for the other side. Boris's escape route came down the street past Rico and Manny. As Boris' car, rapidly picking up speed, got near Rico's rental car Boris saw them running for the car doors, recognized Rico and brought up his gun, slowing his car at the same time.

"Take cover!" shouted Rico. He hit the ground. Manny was already in the passenger seat. He ducked onto the floor as bullets flew into the side of the car. One came through the open driver's window and whanged through the closed right-side rear window. Then Boris was gone, racing down the street.

Rico got the car started, flung it around in a U-turn and gave chase. "Manny, you okay?"

"Goddamnit, Morgan, I'm okay, but I got shot at! It ain't no fun!"

"Call 911 and get the cops to Ginny's place. And hang on!"

Boris Luftin raced around the posh neighborhood in the coming twilight and took a road that ultimately led toward the Chattahoochee Forest to the northeast. He had a good start and knew where he was going, blowing through stoplights and stop signs like he owned the road.

Rico had to take it easy, not knowing the area at all. Manny knew the area slightly, but was little help because he was not driving.

They followed Boris for ten minutes or more, barely able to keep up with him. Sometimes all they had to follow was his taillights in the far distance. Not many other cars were on the road, a blessing, thought Rico.

Finally they got somewhat clear of the residential areas and began to hit slightly more open country. Rico was able to draw closer, though Boris' car, a Maserati, was by far the faster.

Far ahead, they saw Boris turn left off the main highway onto a side street heading north. When they arrived at the corner they saw it was a narrow road. At the side of the road was a sign announcing a camping area ahead. Manny recognized the road. "Rico, this is a dead-end. Ends at the forest up ahead. There's a parking lot for campers, no way out but to turn around and come back."

"How far down does this road end?"

"Less than a mile. I know it well. I used to come camping here with my daughter when she was a kid."

They drove slowly along the narrow road, which headed into thick trees.

At the end of the road they found Boris's car parked in the lot next to several other cars of late-night hikers or overnight campers. There was no sign of Boris. Rico held up his hand for silence. In the deepening shadows of the coming night they heard some noises as of someone hurrying along the trail leading from the parking lot into the dense, now completely dark, woods.

It was after sundown, the light quickly fading, and Rico didn't have a flashlight. Manny had a small pocket LED on his keychain and that was it.

"Manny, I've gotta try to catch him. You don't have to come along. You could get shot."

"Let's go, Rico. I've got the only flashlight and you can't have it!"

"Do you have any idea where this trail goes?" Rico asked as they hurried along the woodland path.

"Yeah, deep into the woods," replied Manny. "That YouTube guy Dave Pearson made some of his excellent camping videos for his 'Fun in the Woods' series in this forest. You can go as far as Tennessee through here if you want to."

"Can Boris double around and get back to the parking lot behind us?"

"Hell yes, if he knows the woods. What're the chances of that?"

"I doubt he's a camper."

But Rico was wrong. Boris knew the woods like his own back yard because he'd camped in them since he was a boy. Boris had the foresight to make all his plans earlier that day, and he knew what he was doing every step of the way. Like the Chinese girls who outfoxed Rico by placing a bug in his hotel room in Casablanca, Boris installed a bug in Ginny's house. He knew he'd find August with Ginny that night. He also knew the two of them planned to sneak off together to Casablanca the following day. He could not, would not, and did not let that happen.

Boris jogged down the trail making noise to draw the followers in after him, and then hid behind a downed stump about fifty yards off the trail and waited. He knew they'd go running by and then he'd go back and get in the car and be in the clear. He didn't have to wait long, but as he lay there his hatred for Rico Morgan came to the fore and grew large. "That bastard Morgan ruined things! He found out way too much. I never thought that prick would learn anything, and Augie didn't do shit to stop his investigations in Casablanca. Should'a shot the bastard a long time ago."

As Boris' hatred grew and Rico and Manny drew near, Boris couldn't resist the temptation. It was a long shot, but Boris took it. He cut loose at Rico from fifty yards away. Luckily for Rico Boris was not a good pistol shot. His bullet didn't come anywhere near the two men. It zinged in front of them into the dirt, a typical jerk-zone hit from an inexperienced shooter.

"Down!" shouted Manny, remembering his combat time in Southeast Asia. He tackled Rico and they hit the dirt of the trail together. Rico had his pistol out, but had no target. "It came from the left, Rico."

"Can't see a friggin' thing. You?"

"Nope! But I hear him running."

"So do I. Shit! He's going back to the car. Or is he? I though the parking lot was over there." Rico pointed left, back down the trail.

"It's actually over there." Manny pointed straight in front of him, at right angles to the path. "He knows a shortcut. The path turns around a bit, but if you know how to do it you can go through some of the brush and thick stuff and down into a little swale, and get to the parking lot pretty fast."

"Then let's get back to the car. Crap! I should've disabled his car, or at least blocked it."

As they ran back along the trail they heard several shots, and then the sound of a car starting and driving away.

When they got to the car both men began cursing. "He shot the fucking tires out. The rotten bastard!" Manny kicked one of the deflated tires and sat on the ground next to it.

"Damn!" said Rico. "He changed cars! His Maserati is right here. It wouldn't have done us any good at all to disable it. Looks like ol' Boris thunk this out well in advance." Rico grabbed his phone and speed dialed Inspector Ralf Raktum. "Ralf, the perp just left us in the dirt. But we don't know what kind of car he's in. He's...er, lemme give you a local who knows where we are." Rico put Manny on the phone to the inspector. Manny told Ralf where they were, and gave the phone back to Rico.

"Rico, I'll send a car to get you guys."

"Hold on, Ralf, we may not need one. Manny, what's up?"

"Gimme a second, Rico, and we can drive outa here."

Manny was up to his elbows under the dash of the Maserati. In short order he got the engine running, and rose from the floor with a smile. "Don't ask how I knew that!"

Rico was still on the phone. "Ralf, we're driving outa here in a fine Maserati. ...Okay, we'll come to Ginny's house. See you soon." Rico put his phone away. "Manny, trust me, I'll never ask how you knew how to do that. But if you want to tell me...??"

"Nope, and I get to drive."

When they got back to Ginny's house Ralf met them out front. "Rico, do you know where Ginny's gone?"

"No. She was here, we heard her screaming, when Boris ran out the front door."

"So you and your friend can verify it was Boris Luftin who was in the house at the time of the murder and presumably shot this guy?"

"Yes. From what we both heard there was an argument, loud voices from three people, then something like, 'I bet you won't do it,' and then, bang-bang-bang. Ginny – it sounded like her but we never actually saw her – said, 'Leave him alone,' or something like that, and Boris said, 'I need this' and ran out of the house a few seconds later."

"The dead man's neck is abraded on the side. Maybe something got snatched from around his neck. Can you come in and ID this guy?"

"I can try. But if it's not August Farchex I'd be surprised."

"Any idea where Ginny went?"

"Negative," replied Rico. "She'd been packing everything. Told me she planned to leave the country – but I told you that already. Maybe she had a ticket to fly. The airport isn't that far from here."

Manny said, "I saw her the past few days driving a VW bug, one of the newer ones. Blue, it was. She always parked it in the driveway next to the house, not in the garage. I don't see the car anywhere but it was here earlier, when the shooting went down."

"Ralf, this is Manny Arkald, my assistant. Manny, Inspector Ralf Raktum."

"Do you run a gym in Atlanta?" asked Ralf.

"Yep, Rico and I go back a long way, and he needed some help, so here I am."

"You give discounts to cops in your gym?"

"No. But come in anyway and I'll see what I can do." Manny grinned.

The body indeed was that of August Farchex. Three shots to the chest killed him. A bloody scrape on the side of his neck indicated the tearing off of something Farchex wore around his neck.

Rico said, "If Boris needed whatever was on this guy's neck, could'a been some kind of pass, a set of keys, something that would let Boris do something easily."

Manny said, "Maybe a magic ring."

"Manny, that's it! It's the odd-looking key to get into the basement vault in Timbuktu!"

"What!?" asked Ralf. "What's in that vault in Timbuktu?"

"Riches beyond belief," replied Rico. "But Boris won't need the key to get in. We blew a hole in the door you can walk through. But he may not know that. What he took could also be the keys to the back door of the old shop. There might even be another vault somewhere that's got more treasures in it, for all we know."

"Gentlemen," said Inspector Ralf Raktum, "thank you for your time. I ain't goin' to Timbuktu! Now I can let forensics know we're done here and they can start to do their job. If you hear anything about Ginny, please let me know, and I'll do likewise."

"Okay, Ralf, but I have a sneakin' suspicion I'm headed back to Idaho without my paycheck from ol' Boris. Also, if you twist Manny's arm just right he'll give you a break on your gym fees."

Manny said, "Sure! I'll just have Rico pay the difference in fees. No problem!"

Manny left the Maserati at Ginny's house, got in his own car and drove Rico to his hotel. They made a beeline for the hotel bar to talk things over. "Manny, I'm buyin'. Get whatever you like, and as much as you like," said Rico. "You can take a cab home, or sleep in the second bed in my room if you overdo things." Rico ordered gin and tonic. He said to the waitress, "Be sure it's Tanqueray Rangpur gin, and Fever Tree low-sugar tonic, if you have them."

Manny ordered Laphroaig Scotch neat with a soda chaser.

"Aargh! Manny, how can you stand that?"

"My ancestors came from the Islay district. The peat bogs get in your blood, I guess."

"So, my friend, what have we accomplished? How do you like the private-eye business? You'll get paid for your time, of course."

"Rico, I don't expect to get paid, and I'll leave all the gumshoeing to you in the future. I'm tired, still shakin' from being shot at, and it looks like we didn't accomplish a goddamned thing. We sat in the car all day, got sore butts, watched stuff happen, couldn't do a thing to change it, someone got killed on our watch, we don't have a clue where the bad guy is or where the eye-witness woman is – herself a murderer – and then the guy who was going to pay you disappears. In short, this sucks."

Rico didn't say anything for a long time. He slugged down his gin and tonic and got another one in front of him before he said anything.

"Manny, you're right. This is an absolute bust. All we got, all I got, was just exactly what you just said, including being screwed for an expensive trip to Casablanca and Timbuktu on top of it all. I know two people killed two other people and both killers got away. I don't think anyone's going to catch either of them, not anytime soon. Ginny could be in Paris, but is probably on her way to Casablanca to see if Farchex left anything there for her that she can pick up and make work. With Augie gone his company, Fortune Technologies, probably won't hold together, not on her word.

"Boris could go there and maybe pull it together and make it work but, inasmuch as he's wanted for murder, I think he's going to lay low in Timbuktu or somewhere else for the foreseeable. I was hired to fix Boris' company's problems. I found the trouble, which I don't think he expected. I was also hired to find the killer of the CEO of the company. I found that killer in Ginny Harumfer, but there's no way to pin it on her.

"It looks like both of these robotics companies are going to die as a result of the actions of the two men who were supposed to be enemies, but were actually friends who turned out, in the end, to be enemies. Each one tried to screw each other, and of course screw Ginny too. Both succeeded in both ways, but Boris came out on top in that he's still alive. I don't know what's going to happen to Luftin-Borlew company here in Atlanta unless someone comes in and does all the right things, and does them fast.

"Bottom line, Manny, I'm ready to crawl back to Idaho, call it a day, sit with my cats, and carefully and thoroughly inspect the contents of certain booze bottles. SHIT!"

"What about the two CIA girls you went to Africa with? Can they help here?"

"No, not really, but I'll call Roxy and let her know what's going on. I'll do that tomorrow. Right now I'm going to have one more drink and call it a day."

CHAPTER 26
Gone

With the disappearance of her husband, now wanted for murder, Becky Luftin quickly gained control of Luftin-Borlew industries. She regretted not having as much time for her beloved golf, but the company soon became her love, and the company's people soon loved her in return.

Becky immediately put out a formal letter to all the companies to which L-B had sold computer-driven machinery over the past two years. Copies went to all the stockholders as well. In it she explained the situation of the bad chips in the company's computers, some details how it happened, and what they could do about it. She recommended the customers inspect each and all of their L-B computers to avoid future problems. It told them exactly what to look for and how to do it. She offered a simple solution: Every company that found an unmarked, or name-defaced, central processing chip in whatever number of computers in which they found them, could notify the Luftin-Borlew company, which would then send the required number of replacement chips of highest quality, all at no cost to the client, with no questions asked. The replacement chips would be made by Intel at half the cost of the original chips, and came with a lifetime warranty.

This effort was met with great support by the company's clients, and in short order the problems were surmounted and the company was back doing proper business. The cost of this 'fix' to the company was minimal compared with the gains in public relations and in future orders.

The debt the L-B company had to Fortune Industries for its large loan of two years earlier lingered unpaid until it was established that Fortune Industries no longer existed, whereupon the debt vanished.

It was near Christmas of that year that Ginny sent full payment to Rico Morgan for all his expenses, and for the agreed-upon fee to determine the problem with the computer chips. Rico didn't get paid for finding the murderer of Ginny's husband because it could not be proven, and besides, no one could find Ginny.

Ginny Harumfer arrived at Farchex's old office in Casablanca to find the Chinese workers, most of them illegal immigrants, had been deported. The company, which she'd hoped to share with August Farchex, was just as dead as he was. There were no orders for new machinery, no workers to make it, only some repair calls which the company had not been able to honor.

No one had been in Farchex's office for nearly a week. All his possessions in the office were untouched by the police. They'd looked at it all, everything in the building in fact, but had no authority to remove or even closely examine any of it.

Ginny sat in his chair, and then realized there'd surely be a bottle of decent booze in the desk. She looked, and quickly found a bottle of Jack Daniels Black Label, nearly full. She found a glass and poured herself a stiff one.

A laptop computer sat closed on top of Augie's desk. It was a fancy one, trimmed in leather, still plugged into the wall. By some chance the power was still on in the building, so the laptop was fully charged. Ginny opened it and turned it on. As she did, she saw a notice of incoming email, the last messages, Ginny supposed, sent to the late August Farchex from...God knew who. She decided to see what they were. But first she had another stiff shot of Black Jack, brushed her long black hair out of her eyes, and propped up her legs on his desk.

She opened the email account, which she happily noted had no password. There was one incoming message, which seemed to be from Augie to himself. She opened it. As soon as she did, all the many images on the computer began to cycle through. The laptop showed them on the screen for maybe half a second. There were dozens of them. Each blinked into life and was replaced by the next in an instant. The computer strained to show each one after the other, then began showing them faster and faster. The screen became dazzling, each image winking on for the briefest part of a second, the order repeating, all fluttering on the computer's 'desktop' behind the window for the email account.

Then Ginny heard a strange sound, a series of discordant notes that were not music, come from the speakers built into the laptop. She heard a hiss coming from inside the fancy laptop as a small gelatin pellet was cooked by a hot wire and burst open, dropping its contents onto the overheated central processing chip. The fan in the computer was already on in a frenzied and futile attempt to cool the runaway thing down. A blast of hot air hit Ginny in the face, and that was the last thing she knew.

A janitor found her a week later. The rats had already begun to reduce her remains to food.

Boris Luftin got clean away. He knew a quick way to get on I-75, so after he shook Rico and Manny he drove to Lovell Field in Chattanooga, where he had a ticket reserved under the name Basil Lewis, using his own initials. He had a cheap but serviceable false driver's license under that name, and that got him on board. He knew the Atlanta police would alert all major airports within a few hundred miles, so he took the precaution to set that up in advance. He flew directly to Miami International.

From Miami he took another big metal bird to Casablanca and, because he needed his passport to enter Morocco, went on that flight under his own name. An hour after his flight landed in Casablanca the Atlanta PD received information from the Miami airport that Luftin was on his way there. By the time the Atlanta PD got data off to Casablanca that they had a killer about to land in their fair city, Boris was checking into a hotel in Timbuktu.

When Mary Teslin's little black-powder bomb went off in that Timbuktu basement, freeing her and Rico and Roxy from their would-be dungeon, luck had it that neither the UN nor the police had been alerted. The UN never found the treasure trove in the basement of the old store in Timbuktu because they never looked into the sound of the blast. Further, when Rico and Mary and Roxy left the old store for the last time they made sure the back door was locked. Because they had been in the basement behind a thick door and thick mud-based walls, most of the sound of the blast went downwards, down the basement stairs, thoroughly ringing Rico's ears on the way. The blast was not loud enough outside the old building to cause the police to investigate.

When Boris Luftin opened the back door of the ancient shop with one of the keys on the chain he'd ripped from around Farchex's neck the first thing he saw was the hole blown in the door the trio had blasted to escape.

"So that's how they got out," he said to himself. "I'll have to fix that." He stepped through the hole and went carefully down the stairs. The lights were still on. The blast never hurt any of the lights except for the one near the top of the stairs just inside the vault door. Farchex had paid the power bill several years in advance, so the power was still running. The lights showed Boris the way.

He paused for a long moment at the foot of the stairs, looking out over the treasure-filled room, the paintings on the wall, the fine art under protective glass cases. "All mine," he intoned softly.

Then he walked slowly among the hundreds of priceless artifacts, collected over the years by himself and by Farchex. They'd traded worthless trinkets for the real stuff, cheated old families out of their heirlooms, sometimes resorted to theft to get an item they wanted but could find no other way of obtaining. Over many years the two men acquired, by hook or by crook, every fine-artistic item they could find that originated in ancient golden Timbuktu. These pieces had untold value because they were fine items by themselves, and more because they had an historic link to the past.

Farchex did most of the gathering, but Boris was often there in the old city to help, and also in Casablanca often enough to help Farchex get what they wanted out of collections and museums that needed a bit of quick cash. They stored it all this basement.

The basement had been an ancient vaulted storage chamber that Farchex read about, years ago, back when he was in college. It used to be a sort of prison, lost to history hundreds of years before. Mention was made in various old texts, the texts actually being part of the grand historic record of Timbuktu. Those documents are treasures of another sort, still mostly held by the families in which the documents had originated.

Farchex found the vault, bought the land and the old shop that stood over it, repaired the vault, cleared out all the sand, reinforced the ceiling, cut some new tunnels to give alternate escape routes, ventilated and wired the whole place, and made the vault into a stunning and totally private museum. Augie supervised the construction and his old college chum Boris provided most of the money for the job. Now it all belonged to Boris Luftin.

Boris moved the couch back against the wall and sat on it, totally at peace. "That bastard tried to cheat me out this," he said. "Now what's he got? The same cold grave he tried to give me. Got what he deserved." Boris leaned back, took a small flask out of his pocket, and had a drink.

What Boris Luftin didn't know was that August X. Farchex didn't give a stinking crap about all the trinkets and treasures in the underground museum. The day before Rico and his friends got trapped underground, Augie fixed up the trap to lock anyone who entered it inside the vault – if they were foolish enough to go down there in the first place. He didn't dream anyone could ever get out. But he wanted to be sure the trap worked.

So he flew his lovely Beechcraft Baron to Mopti, languished there a while, and then flew back to Timbuktu to see if the trap had been sprung. It had. And then had been unceremoniously blown apart by the charge of black powder thoughtfully provided by Mary Teslin. Rico and the two CIA women were long gone when Farchex found the blown door. He entered the vault, cautiously of course, and went down and looked at all the goodies. Then he cursed roundly.

"All this useless crap," he said. "A bunch of stuff worth maybe a few million bucks. Who gives a shit?! Not me. They're only worth what you can get for 'em. I'm so sick of sitting on 'em and looking at 'em, I hope I never see 'em again."

Then he sat on the sofa couch and thought about things for a long time. "Maybe Morgan will come back," he said to himself. "He might like to have some of this. Maybe Luftin will try to screw me and come back here to gloat, maybe play with the swords, look at the paintings. Okay, that does it! I'll take the Van Gogh and the other good one, a few of the best of the old guns, maybe a sword or two. Luftin can have the rest. I hate that carved-ivory crap. Better left on the elephant, as far as I'm concerned."

He though about it some more. Then he removed a select few of the items and took them up to his car, went back down and spent a few hours there, fussing with his beloved robotics, and with the electronics. He rummaged around here and there for a long time, setting things in some kind of order.

"That should do it," he said. August X. Farchex left the basement museum and the ancient store for the last time and headed for the airport – and his fatal meeting with the bullets from Boris Luftin's gun.

Boris Luftin pulled one of the swords off the wall and admired its jeweled handle. Rubies, emeralds, a diamond or two, all set in gold. He looked for the Van Gogh but didn't find it. Then he noticed a few of the matchlocks were missing, including the one with the ivory stock. He went to a glass case that had some of the finest ivory carvings in it. Most of the intricately carved, delicate white items were there, but the miniature 'Pietà,' the body of Jesus on his mother's lap, which August Farchex knew was Boris' all-time favorite of the ivory carvings, was missing. "What the heck?!" he said. Boris Luftin lifted the glass top off the case....

The blast shook the headquarters of the UN building across town. Pieces of wood and shards of mud bricks from the old store rained down for many seconds. When the UN people got there all they saw was a huge depression in the ground where the old store had been.

CHAPTER 27
Coolin' It

The beautiful guitar notes of Saturday Sun and the clear, high voice of Alex Hedley cut through the soft night air as he sang "Seagull."

Do you give much?
Do you take more?
Do you know what's good?
Build your tower, on the ladder,
But I've no reason to climb for you.

Rico sat outdoors at Mary Teslin's brother's house in New Brunswick, New Jersey, sipping a Margarita in the cool of the evening and soaking in the intensely emotional music. Outdoor speakers softly played the enchanting sounds to the three friends. A barbecue sputtered with hot dogs, some fried chicken, fries warming in a pan. The cooler had beer and ice, and various bottles of spirits and mixers were on a handy table. Night had fallen, and there was peace in the air.

Mary's brother John was gone with his wife to celebrate their anniversary, and their son Sammy Teslin was left with Mary.

Mary and Roxy had a week off from their work at CIA, and Rico, having phoned Roxy from Atlanta, had been invited to spend time with them.

"Roxy, if you're sure it won't be an imposition on you or Mary, I'd far rather go to New Jersey than Idaho right now."

Roxy put Mary on the phone. "Rico, for the love of God come here. Tell us all the story, what happened, and the whole works of it. You will not be in the way. My brother John, a math professor at Rutgers, is off for a couple weeks with his wife celebrating their wedding anniversary. They're in Texas. Granddad lives there, and they went to visit and hang out. Their son, my nephew Sammy, is here and so is Roxy. We'd love to have you."

Rico had said his goodbyes to Manny the night before at the bar. That night, Rico went to his room, stared out the window, and finally collapsed on the bed, spiritually and mentally exhausted. The next morning, nursing a slight hangover, he phoned Roxy and then made plans to fly from Atlanta to New Brunswick, home of Rutgers University.

Roxy met him at Newark airport and drove him to Mary's house, where he met Mary's nephew, Sammy Teslin. Rico spoke to him as he did to all young people in their early teens, which was as though the youngster was an adult. "Hi, Sam! I'm Rico."

"Hi, Mr. Morgan. Pleased to meet you." He shook hands with a sturdy grip.

Mary said to her nephew, "Sammy, why don't you go play that new computer game Roxy got for you."

"Can't I stay and listen?"

"Well, my boy, the talk might get pretty rowdy."

"Heck," said Rico, "I can tone it down if you ladies can. I don't mind if Sam hears what we all did. Might be interesting."

"Ok, as long as we don't talk too much about what happened to the fat man in Atlanta."

So the four of them sat in the back yard and ate hot dogs and potato chips, drank this and that, and chatted into the evening. As the sun settled in the west and the drinks eased the atmosphere, talk turned to their travels and the consequences of them.

Mary said, "Rico, we just got word at the office that the CIA let it leak to the Chinese that the miserable piece of dog crap called Miles Drapcox was responsible for the destruction of the new Chinese factory there. The Company also let it be known that August Farchex paid Drapcox to do it, so the Chinese were not happy to learn about the many workers from their country employed by Mr. Farchex. I guess they'll get their hands slapped once they go back to China, if they ever go back."

"I think they might. There's no one to run the company unless Ginny can do it, wherever she might be. I'm guessing the Chinese workers were illegal immigrants, and if the company shuts down, they'll have to go back to China."

"And face the music," said Roxy.

"Speaking of music," said Rico as the end of "Seagull" faded away, "do you have any more stuff by Saturday Sun? That's really outstanding."

"Their album '*Orixé*' is on the player," said Mary. "You'll hear all it has."

"I love that guy's voice, said Rico. "What's his name? Alex Hedley? And you say he's British? Where's Swanage? Er, never mind. Okay, thanks. So, why did you two go to Australia in the first place?"

Roxy answered, "The Agency didn't like Drapcox ever since he took office. They suspected he was crooked, so that's why we were sent there. We needed to find any dirt on him and get him ousted. He got ousted. Yay."

Mary asked, "Rico, whatever possessed these two guys to get together to destroy one of their companies? Do you have any idea?"

Roxy added, "Good question. How did all that start?"

Rico told them, "I have a vague idea. Some time back when I first started this investigation I got a phone call from my friend Bruce Nourse, the computer guru in Ann Arbor. In his vast exploration of the guts of computers over the years and what they can and cannot do, he learned a fascinating true story. He told it to me, which gave me a clue as to what might have gone on with the two crooks. The gist of his information was that some years ago a well-known chip maker produced a master chip for desk-top computers that worked just fine. The company then made another run of them, but soon mathematicians who were using them to solve deep, complex equations found out the answers they were getting were incorrect. They checked their math results with those done on other computers that had chips by different makers and, Lo! the answers were coming out right. The famous chip maker finally admitted, Bruce learned, that there was a glitch in the making of the second batch of their chip, and the next batch again gave the correct answers all the time.

"Bruce suggested something like this might have happened with Fortune Tech in Casablanca. They found a glitch in a new batch of their chips. Crooked minds always look to see what they can get out of stuff like that, what advantage it might give them to use the bad chips rather than just zinging them and starting over. Farchex discovered his bad chips worked for a time and then would do odd things, totally out of control. He let Boris Luftin know. The two men were working in tandem on various projects back then, and they realized that flaw was something they could exploit to ruin a company. They needed a patsy to take the fall from their use of the bad chips.

Young Sammy asked, "What good would it do to ruin some company? Did they want to do it just for fun?"

"Well, Sam, it came down to money. I suspect this guy Boris was tired of running his company. He wanted to retire but retirement was long years off. He could sell the company, but the company had a huge financial debt. He realized if the company failed he'd make out with a huge payoff because of the master insurance program he'd set up for his operation some years before. He'd get far more money from the insurance outfit if his company failed, than he'd get out of a fair sale. So his own company became the patsy.

"When things started to go bad his CEO, Herbert Harumfer, looked into it and contacted me, and you know the story from there on. For Sam's benefit, the situation involved murder, fraud, payoffs, shootings, and the hard work of your aunt and her friend to run down a couple of crooks. They did a fine job."

Roxy coughed into her hand, "Rico helped!"

"At any rate, as you know now, we proved Fortune Technologies was indeed guilty of making and installing these faulty chips into Luftin-Borlew's machinery in a calculated effort by Boris Luftin to destroy his own company."

"Man!" said Sammy. "What a story!" He looked thoughtful for a while, and suddenly said, Hey, Mr. Morgan, come and see this new video game I got from Miss Roades. You'll love it!"

Rico went with Sammy to see the game, and the two women followed, curious. Sammy explained what it did and how it was supposed to go, and then said, I'm eager to try it, but I don't want to miss any of your stories."

Rico said, "That's all right. We'll save all the good stories for when you get done with your game.

"Okay, sir, so will you excuse me while I try this?"

Rico glanced at Roxy, caught her eye. They smiled wistfully at each other, both knowing they might never see each other again after this brief meeting in New Jersey. Rico looked back at the young man.

"Play it!" said Rico. "Play it, Sam!"

CASABLANCA CAPER

CREATED BY SHEEP CREEK PUBLISHING, NORTH FORK, ID 83466

www.ingramcontent.com/pod-product-compliance
Lightning Source LLC
Chambersburg PA
CBHW051456170626
46811CB00002B/500

* 9 7 8 1 7 3 3 1 3 5 2 2 1 *